D0483481

Matt stirred restlessly in his saddle, realizing that he seemed always to be looking for something. He'd never gotten over losing Becky. For years his life had revolved around his sister, and when she'd married, his life lost its purpose. Could he be lonely? _Admit it, you've always been lonely_ ....At thirty-eight, he wasn't apt to find anyone to love him, so he might as well stifle such thoughts.

Unity tiptoed to the hallway door. Rather than interfering with her plans, perhaps the noise of the storm would cloak the sound of her departure. After opening the door, she paused on the threshold and surveyed the room she'd shared with Samuel Whitley, and she shuddered at the memories the room evoked.... She waited for occasional flashes of lightning to illuminate her way along the sea wall. "The tides of time wash over my soul, scattering doubt and fear." Somewhere in the past she'd read those words, and tonight they brought comfort. The course of action she was initiating prompted many doubts, but she had no other choice.

True happiness seems to elude both Matt Miller and Unity Spencer, until they meet amidst the passion and excitement of the California Gold Rush. But before too long, each must face _Unbidden Secrets_ that threaten to destroy their deep, ardent love.

For your reading pleasure, look for these Meadowsong Romances:

from Irene Brand:
Freedom's Call
The Touchstone

from Barbara Masci:
Forbidden Legacy
Captured Heart
Stolen Heritage

BY Irene B. Brand:

The Touchstone
Freedom's Call
Unbidden Secrets

UNBIDDEN SECRETS

IRENE B. BRAND

Fleming H. Revell Company
Tarrytown, New York

Scripture quotations in this volume are from the King James Version of the Bible.

Library of Congress Cataloging-in-Publication Data

Brand, Irene B., date
     Unbidden secrets / Irene B. Brand.
         p.   cm.
     ISBN 0-8007-5388-7
     I. Title.
     PS3552.R2917U5   1991
     813'.54—dc20
                                                                    90-19227
                                                                    CIP

All rights reserved. No part of this publication may be reproduced, stored in a retrieval system, or transmitted in any form or by any means—electronic, mechanical, photocopy, recording or any other—except for brief quotations in printed reviews, without the prior permission of the publisher.

Copyright © 1991 by Irene B. Brand
Published by the Fleming H. Revell Company
Tarrytown, New York 10591
Printed in the United States of America

TO
our friends
Allen and Naomi McKinney

UNBIDDEN SECRETS

1

*U*nity's hands gripped the windowsill as she listened to the angry surf beating against the shore. Lightning pierced the sky; thunder rumbled in the distance; and rain pelted the window. Taking advantage of a flash of lightning, she glanced at the heavy watch hanging around her neck: almost ten o'clock.

Picking up a valise, she tiptoed to the hallway door. Rather than interfering with her plans, perhaps the noise of the storm would cloak the sound of her departure. After she'd opened the door, she paused on the threshold and surveyed the room she'd shared with Samuel Whitley. She shuddered at the memories the room evoked. Leaving surreptitiously meant that she had to abandon most of her personal possessions, but that was a small price to pay for liberation from her husband's family.

Creeping down the stairs, she crossed the drawing room to a door that she had unlocked earlier in the day. It moved at the touch of her hand, and Unity breathed a prayer of thanks that the butler hadn't checked that opening before he retired for the night. With one hand she pulled up the hood of her cloak; then Unity stepped out into the dark, blustery night. Groping in the blackness, she waited for occasional flashes of lightning to illuminate her way along the sea wall.

The Whitleys had built their home overlooking this rugged section of Rhode Island coast in eighteen hundred, almost a half century ago. One of the few pleasures Unity had experienced while she lived here was to stand on the wall and watch the powerful waves as they assaulted the heavy stones. Hearing the deafening attack of the waves splashing around her, she knew the ocean was at high tide tonight.

"The tides of time wash over my soul, scattering doubt and fear." Somewhere in the past she'd read those words, and tonight they brought comfort. The course of action she was initiating prompted many doubts, but she had no other choice.

Not for the first time, Unity wondered what she would do if the coach wasn't there. She had told her sister to have someone meet her at the crossroads between the Whitley mansion and Newport at half past ten o'clock on the first of April. If Margaret hadn't received her message, she didn't know what she'd do. Quickly she offered up a prayer. No, God had not deserted her. A sense of comfort came upon her.

The storm abated suddenly, and the moon peeped from behind an inky cloud. The roadway showed up more plainly now, and with a lighter heart, Unity hurried forward. After another mile, when she saw the Spencer coach waiting at the crossroads, she broke into a run.

Stoddard, her father's coachman, stood beside the door, and a nervous sobbing laugh escaped Unity's throat. Seeing him standing there, waiting to serve her as he'd done for so many years, brought a wave of emotion over Unity. When Deborah Jenkins stepped from the coach and held out her arms, Unity threw herself upon the woman and sobbed as she never had at the death of her father or the drowning of her husband.

"You're soaked, Miss Unity. Step inside the coach, and we'll be on our way," Deborah said softly.

Stoddard helped the two women enter the coach, and in a few minutes the hooves of the four horses pitched mud all around their vehicle as the coachman lashed the animals forward.

"I didn't expect you to come, Deborah, but thank you."

"Not come?" Deborah snorted. "And have you roaming around this country with nobody but Stoddard!

"We're planning to drive for several hours, then put up at an inn and travel to Boston at a more leisurely pace," she explained.

"Is Margaret angry with me?"

"No, but she is puzzled over why you had to sneak away from the Whitleys. Surely they wouldn't have prevented you from returning to your home for a visit?"

"It isn't for a visit. I never intend to return to the Whitleys." Even in the darkness, Unity could sense Deborah's appraising glance. "When we arrive in Boston, I'll write and let them know, but I wanted to avoid the unpleasantness of telling them in person. Deborah, these three months of my marriage have seemed as long as a lifetime. Surely if father had possessed any idea of what these people are like, he would have found another husband for me."

"We'll talk about it later, Miss Unity," she soothed her. "Why don't you try to rest now?"

They reached the inn long after midnight, but since ar-

11

rangements for their lodging had already been made, Deborah and Unity soon found themselves in a bedroom.

"Could you bring some warm water and a light meal, please, and also take some food and drink to the coachman?" Unity asked the landlady, who had shown them to their room.

When the woman left, Deborah said, "The first thing is to rid you of those wet clothes, and I'll give you a good rubdown."

"I left most of my clothing behind, but I have a nightgown in my bag."

A slow-burning blaze in the fireplace warmed the room. Deborah spread Unity's garments near the flames to dry and pulled a small table close to the fire. While they ate the cheese and bread the landlady provided Unity laid her hand on Deborah's rough one. This good-tempered, kindly woman with grayish hair and brown eyes had been the only mother she'd known. Unity's mother had died in childbirth, so Unity and her sister Margaret had grown up under Deborah's care.

"Oh, Deborah, how good to have you back with me. You're always there to lean on."

"Why do you need to lean on me now?" Seeing the trouble in Unity's face, she asked, "Do you want to talk or go to bed?"

"Why not go to bed *and* talk? This room will become cold when that fire dies down."

Unity climbed into the high bed and wrapped the heavy comforter around her shoulders. She faced Deborah, who reclined in a similar bed to her right.

"After my marriage, I discovered the Whitleys made their money by piracy. Samuel's father operated off a distant island in the Caribbean, until a few years ago, when United States and British authorities made it too hot for him. I think the family still plunders foreign boats behind the back of the law—when they can get away with it. Their home is decorated with items they've already stolen. They make no bones about it, brag about their unlawfulness."

"Miss Unity! Piracy in this day and age?"

"I know, I could hardly accept it myself, when I first found out. I thought the sailor who told me was lying. But I've found proof—documents—though I could never get my hands on them long enough to bring them to the authorities."

"We could tell from your letters that all wasn't well, but we'd never have guessed that. What was your father doing, marrying you into such a family?"

"It's all true, nonetheless. They're such godless people—made fun of my Christian beliefs Samuel was the worst. I avoided the rest of his family, when possible, but I couldn't avoid him." She shuddered, remembering the sadistic treatment she'd suffered at his hands.

Deborah, noting the shudder, said quickly, "What caused his death?"

"He drowned." Despite her pain, Unity felt horror sweep over her. "He and two others went fishing in a small sloop. Gale-force winds blew that day, and even Samuel's father tried to keep him from going, but no one could tell my husband anything. They didn't return that night, and the next day the tide brought in the body of one sailor and portions of the wrecked boat."

"But not Samuel's body?"

"No, his body hasn't been recovered, and his parents finally accepted his death and went into mourning. I pity them, for Samuel was their only child, and they can't turn to God for comfort. After the way he treated me, I can't feel much except a great relief to be rid of him. How could I have endured a lifetime as Samuel Whitley's wife?"

"But why leave in this manner? Would they have prevented your leaving?"

"Oh, no, I think they'll be glad to know I'm gone. When Samuel's father learned that I retained control of my inheritance, he would have turned me out anytime. That's not the reason I left." She paused. "I guess I may as well tell you. I'm going to have a baby. That child would be Samuel's heir, so his father will want custody. How could I legally prevent them from taking the child? The only way I know to keep the child safe is if they never know one exists."

"If his body hasn't been found, your husband might still show up. He'll want his child."

"I don't believe there's a chance in a million that he could be alive, but if he is, he'll get *my* child over my dead body." Unity halted again. "You know I'd never do this if there were another way. But I have to do something!

"You remember we wondered why Samuel had waited until he was approaching middle age to marry?" Unity's face flamed as she continued, "He didn't marry because he prefers boys to women."

"Miss Unity!" Deborah whispered, aghast.

"I hate to admit this, but it's true. I suppose I'd lived a sheltered life, for I had no idea such relationships existed, but once I'd found out, Samuel constantly taunted me about it."

Deborah wept silently, and Unity said, "Someone had to know, and I can trust you more than anyone else to help me conceal the birth of my child from the Whitleys."

"You won't be difficult to trace, if they're so inclined."

"I'm hoping they won't want to keep in touch with me, but I'll do anything I can to prevent a child of mine from being reared in such an environment."

After Deborah went to sleep, Unity lay awake for a long

time. Was she going to like living with Margaret, who, since their father's recent death, had moved into the family home? Where else could she go? At least until her child was born, she felt the necessity of being with family.

How was Margaret going to take the news of Unity's pregnancy? Three years older than Unity, Margaret had been married for eight years to Isaac Smith, and her inability to conceive a child had eaten at her like wormwood. She had always been jealous of Unity, and in spite of Unity's unfortunate marriage, Margaret might well resent the fact that her sister could produce a baby when she couldn't.

Unity's wrath against her father flared. How dared he use his daughters as pawns in his ambition to own the largest shipping business in Boston? Isaac Smith had inherited a fleet of vessels from his uncle, so their father had sought him as a husband for Margaret. However, Isaac was a good man, and apart from childlessness, the couple's union had been pleasant enough.

As Unity had developed into a tall, slender, beautiful woman, Margaret had become prey to fits of jealousy. Unity's reddish-brown hair surrounded a face highlighted with twinkling brown eyes and a short, pert nose. Full lips looked always ready for laughter.

Physically the sisters resembled each other in some ways, for Margaret's hair and eyes were brown, but her set, grim face and her uplifted, arrogant chin set the tone for her personality.

Unity had been barraged with suitors, but her father had turned them all away until Samuel Whitley came to Boston. In Samuel's good-looking face, a determined chin bore a deep cleft, almost giving the appearance of a scar. After moving to Rhode Island, Unity had learned the cleft was a Whitley marking. Every male Whitley she saw had it.

Samuel had been extremely sure of himself, and once he started to pursue Unity, his persistence might have won her, if it hadn't been for his eyes. Whatever emotions the rest of his face revealed, Samuel's sullen blue eyes never smiled. Unity had opposed the wedding, although she'd finally acquiesced to her father's wishes.

Three days after their wedding, before the couple had left Boston for the Whitley's mansion along the coast of Rhode Island, Unity's father had died. Samuel might have made her a somewhat acceptable husband, had he decided to live at peace with her and simply let Unity go her own way, but when the solicitor read the last will and testament of Robert Spencer, any amicability he might have shown vanished.

Robert Spencer had already taken Isaac Smith, Margaret's husband, into partnership in Spencer Shipping, and upon her father's death, his will stated that Unity was to assume complete control of her half of the estate. Realizing that Unity possessed the intellect he had hoped for in a son, Robert Spencer had trained her to operate the business, if that should ever be her lot. He didn't want her hands tied by a husband who might seek to change Spencer policy.

For several years Robert's younger brother, John, had operated the Pacific end of Spencer Shipping, but he wanted to be released from his duties. Now her father's plan that Unity and Samuel would travel to California to assume control of the western half of the Spencer trade had been doomed. "What's he take me for?" Samuel had shouted when he heard of it. "Just married you to me so he could get Whitley money, huh? I won't be a lackey for any woman. Somebody else can run his company. We're not going to California."

The day the will was read, Samuel had taken Unity to

Newport with him, and the anger he felt against Robert Spencer he had vented upon his daughter. No matter what happened, Unity knew that life with Margaret and Isaac would be heaven, compared to what she'd endured at Samuel's hands.

"God," she prayed as her lids grew heavy. "My future is in Your hands."

Unity slept, but her dreams were troubled. She imagined herself drifting with the tide. At first, she was lashed and driven against the rocks of the harsh New England coast, but suddenly the seas calmed, and she drifted peacefully toward another shore. The waves were warm and balmy; sea otters swam playfully around her; and she looked upon a coast of azure water lined with rows of pines and oaks and a glistening ribbon of sand.

Unity was sorry to learn that Isaac Smith wasn't at home, for she'd looked forward to having his advice on how to conceal her child from the Whitleys. Margaret welcomed her warmly enough, generously assuring Unity that she could stay with them as long as she wanted to. Unity soon resettled into the household she'd left only a few months before.

Recently Isaac had set sail on a long voyage, and since it would be several months before his return, Unity went to her father's solicitor, William Bagley, with an unusual request.

"I want you to initiate action to secure me a divorce from Samuel," she told the lawyer forthrightly.

"It seems like an underhanded action against a dead man," he remonstrated. "If he's dead, what's the reason for a divorce?"

"Do you ever read the Bible, Mr. Bagley?"

"Of course," he sputtered, incensed.

Taking a New Testament from her reticule, Unity said, "Read Romans chapter one, verses twenty-six and twenty-seven, and you'll see why I want no ties with Samuel Whitley, living or dead."

The solicitor's eyes bulged, and his face purpled as he read. He refused to meet her eyes.

"Samuel's body was never recovered, Mr. Bagley. While I have no reason to believe he survived that wreck, I remember the fate of President Jackson and his wife, a few years ago. It nearly ruined their marriage when she learned she was still legally tied to her first husband. I don't know that I'll ever marry again, but I don't want any possibility of the reappearance of Samuel to tie me to him, and I want no ties between my family and his."

"Have you considered that as their daughter-in-law, the Whitleys might name you in their will?"

"Mr. Bagley, *I* know how the Whitleys made their fortune, and I don't want any of it."

Mr. Bagley snorted and harrumphed, but he finally agreed to secure the divorce, although Unity knew he would never have done so if he'd known she would bear a child. Unity left the office with a sense of relief. After her union with Samuel, she had no desire to remarry, but she couldn't admit to Mr. Bagley that, legally free of Samuel, she might be able to thwart the Whitleys, should they learn about her baby.

Two weeks after Unity arrived in Boston, Margaret entered her bedroom one night. Unity mistrusted the calculating look on her sister's face, when she asked, "When did you say your child is due?"

"Deborah thinks it will be around the first of October."

Margaret counted on her fingers and muttered, "That should work then." She sat on the bed and took Unity's hand. "I know you're afraid that the Whitleys will try to take your baby, and I think I've come up with the answer."

"What?" Unity asked suspiciously.

"Give the child to me." As Unity's startled gaze lifted to hers, Margaret said, "Now just a minute, listen to me. Nobody knows you're expecting this child, except the two of us and Deborah. Before you start showing, we can go to Isaac's farm and stay there until the baby is born. When we come back to Boston, I'll be the child's mother. No one else needs to know."

"And Isaac?"

"It's been one of the greatest disappointments of my life that I can't give him a son, and I want him to think the child is mine. He left here two months ago for the Sandwich Islands. The baby will be born before he returns. I tell you, it's the safest way. If the Whitleys find out you've borne Samuel's child, they'll take it."

Unity hid her face in uplifted hands. "Either way, it seems I'll lose my child."

"But you *won't* lose him if you give him to me," Margaret persisted. "You'll continue to live here in the house; you can help with his upbringing. You'd be his aunt— almost as good as being his mother—and eventually he'd inherit all of the Spencer fortune. I tell you, it's the only way."

When Deborah learned of Margaret's proposal, she opposed it instantly. "It won't work, Miss Unity," she said heatedly. "When you start manipulating babies around, it causes trouble. For one thing, it's not fair to Mr. Isaac to deceive him, and it won't be good for the little one. These things always come out, one way or another, and I don't think the Lord will be pleased with such a plan."

Unity had her doubts, but when she discovered that the Whitleys had contacted William Bagley in an attempt to find her, she felt she had no choice. As she balanced giving her child to Margaret against the chance that the amoral Whitleys might gain his or her custody, she chose to go along with Margaret's deception. In spite of her displeasure, Deborah agreed to help them, but she warned, "Miss Unity, you should know you can't always trust your sister. You'll be sorry you did this."

Accustomed to being active, the months of seclusion Unity spent at the Smith's isolated farm nearly drove her to distraction. She always had Deborah for company and came to rely on the good woman more than ever. Even as the new life grew within her, Unity conceived a boundless love for it that amazed her. How could she possibly give away this child?

Margaret frequently went into Boston to check on the family business, and during those times she padded her garments to indicate her "pregnancy." While Unity became more morose over the possibility of losing the child, Margaret went about happier than Unity had ever seen her.

Their scheme seemed to work well enough until the time came for the delivery. With all her skill, Deborah couldn't help. The labor began smoothly, but the child refused to come. As Unity became weaker, Deborah said, "She needs help that I can't give her. Send for a doctor; surely there's one in the village."

"But that will ruin everything!" Margaret protested. "I don't want *anyone* to know that I didn't bear the child."

Deborah turned on her angrily, pointing to Unity, who had just suffered a birth pang that caused her to bolt upright in the bed and gasp for breath. "Don't you ever think of anyone but yourself? If she suffers much more, you won't have a baby or a sister either. Send for a doctor."

By the time the local doctor, Micah Dilcher, arrived, the boy child had finally forced his way into the world, but Deborah was relieved to have a trained medic tend to the child and to Unity. Margaret fretted all the time the doctor was in the house, however, and Unity shared her relief when they saw the last of this large, florid man with clumsy hands, who peered at her from a twitching left eye.

Levi Smith was five months old when Isaac returned from his sea voyage, and his delight that Margaret had borne him a child partly recompensed Unity for the deception that still nagged at her spirit. Unity and Isaac had always been friends, and she was pleased she could contribute to his happiness.

The first months of Levi's life had been happy for Unity, in spite of her weakness from the cruel delivery. Unity found it a pleasure to look after the child, but with Isaac's homecoming, Margaret decided they must have a wet nurse. "For what if Isaac should see you nursing him?" she said. "He would know we'd deceived him."

Gradually Margaret tried to assume more and more care of the child, but right from the first, Levi fretted and cried when Margaret held him. If he passed from her arms to Unity's, in a few moments the child gurgled with pleasure.

"You can't fool a baby," Deborah said with obvious satisfaction. "The little one knows his mother."

Tensions grew between Unity and Margaret concerning care of Levi and over the fact that Isaac discussed the shipping business with Unity. "After all, you're a partner in this company," he said. "You should know what's going on." But Margaret's jealousy seemed to grow daily.

Isaac's biggest concern was the California trade, now

that Unity and Samuel wouldn't be moving west to assume that responsibility. "Your uncle John likes living on his father-in-law's rancho and anticipates going there to manage the place. I suppose Margaret and I could move to California and you could manage the business here."

Margaret and Unity both protested at once, but for different reasons. Margaret didn't want to live among the heathen, as she termed the Mexicans, and although Unity had already determined that she had to move away from the Smiths, she didn't want a continent to separate her from her son. Living across town would be bad enough.

When Unity made known her intentions of leaving, Isaac protested, "By no means. This is your home."

On the other hand, Deborah pressured her to move. "Go, and take the child with you. Margaret can't handle him, and he's going to be ruined in her care."

Unity was on the verge of telling the truth and following her advice, when Isaac suffered a stroke. In a few weeks, fair-haired Isaac, who had come home from his sea voyage broad-shouldered and tanned, spoke in a faltering voice and stared at them from a cadaverous face. Although the doctor assured Margaret that he would recover completely, Unity feared that if she were to reveal the truth about Levi, it might kill Isaac.

But Unity couldn't take Margaret's animosity any longer, and in spite of the promises her sister had made before Levi's birth, Margaret forestalled Unity's attempts to be alone with her child.

Again Unity dreamed of a sheet of azure water lined with rows of pines and oaks and a glistening ribbon of sand, and after she listened to Isaac sing the praises of California, she wondered if her dream had been about that faraway land. So one morning, when she went to see

Isaac, she set aside her confusion and said, "I've decided *I'll* go to California to manage the family business."

He reached for her hand and said in his halting speech, "That may be best; you know more about Spencer Shipping than I do. I can see the situation here isn't good for you, and I've been worrying about whom we could send to relieve John of that responsibility."

"I'll need some advice on how to travel."

"You can't go alone. Perhaps Deborah can travel with you."

"Oh, no, I wouldn't ask her." If she had to leave Levi behind in Boston, she wanted Deborah to look after him. Obviously Margaret had no love for the child.

"But you must have female company on such a trip," Isaac insisted.

After Unity went to her room, she looked at her drawn face in the mirror. Once people had often remarked about the fact that she laughed so much. How long had it been since she'd laughed? Certainly not since her marriage to Samuel Whitley. Would she ever be happy again?

What kind of mother would actually consider going off and leaving her child? *I'm a harried mother*, she answered herself. *And I'm only seeking what's best for my child.*

Even now she had nightmares about her son growing up in the Whitley mansion. After their first attempt to discover her whereabouts, the Whitleys had made no efforts to contact Unity. But what if they discovered that a child had been born? Would they realize he could be hers?

"Maybe I haven't made all the right decisions so far, Lord," she prayed. "But I do want my son to know Jesus. Nothing looks right now. So if it's Your will for me to leave all this behind, make my way plain."

2

Matt Miller lounged carelessly against the adobe wall of the fort. To a casual observer he didn't seem to have a care in the world, but inwardly the schooner captain seethed. John Sutter still hadn't paid him for the herd of cattle he'd brought from Oregon.

That's the worst part of doing business with Sutter, Matt thought. *He is* always *short of money.*

I suppose I shouldn't complain; hasn't Sutter entertained me royally in the week I've been here? he tried to excuse the man. But patience wasn't one of Matt's virtues, and again longings to return home rose in him. Noting that the sun neared its zenith, Matt calculated he shouldn't have much longer to wait, if Sutter kept his word. The trader had assured him he'd have the money this afternoon.

On the trail along the Sacramento River, a bearded man appeared, rapidly walking toward the fort. Recognizing James Marshall, whom he'd known for several years, and seeking a diversion from his thoughts, Matt called out a greeting.

Marshall glanced up furtively, raised his hand, and hurried through the gate of the fort. Thoughtfully, Matt followed him and watched Marshall enter Sutter's apartments.

"I suppose that means Sutter won't see me for a while," he muttered, vowing this would be the last time he'd bother with the Swiss emigrant. Still, it was a good market when Sutter finally paid up, and there weren't many people in California interested in buying the purebred cattle his brother-in-law, Maurie, raised on his ranch in Oregon.

Leaning against a post on the porch of Sutter's store, Matt looked around him. John Sutter had done well for himself since he'd arrived in California nine years ago, in eighteen thirty-nine. When Sutter had secured this land grant from the Mexicans, there had been nothing here but a wilderness, but now he operated a tannery, a gristmill, a distillery, and shops housing weavers, blacksmiths, and carpenters.

Prepared for trouble that hadn't come, Sutter had constructed the fort of adobe walls eighteen feet high and three feet thick. Three cannon mounted on the bastioned corners served as a warning. Outside the walls, Sutter ran thousands of cattle, and his many servants cultivated large tracts of grain and nurtured a ten-acre orchard.

A half hour later when Sutter's bookkeeper breezed out of the building, Matt called, "Hey, buddy, can you tell me how long Marshall is going to be in there?"

The man's eyes snapped angrily. "I don't know. Accused me of spying on them. I went in to ask the boss a question, and Marshall acted like a crazy man. Said that he'd told Sutter to lock the door."

Matt looked thoughtful. "What did you hear? What were they doing?"

"I heard nothing. They were looking at a pile of gravel on the table, but Marshall threw his hat over it when I went into the room."

"What's Marshall been doing? I hadn't seen him around the fort until today."

"Building a sawmill for Sutter up in the mountains along the American River. He's had a crew up there for six months."

Staring after the bookkeeper, his black eyes glinting speculatively behind heavy eyelids, Matt whistled tunelessly, puzzled about Marshall's strange behavior. He walked to the bank of the river and went aboard his three-masted schooner, where four sailors mended some rigging.

"When are we pulling out of here?" asked Sid Green, a scrawny man in his late forties.

"As soon as Sutter pays me."

Green snorted. "I believe the captain likes to put on a big show—don't believe he has the money he pretends to have."

"Well, he has twenty of my brother-in-law's cows, and I don't intend to leave here until he pays for them."

Matt walked back inside the fort and waited another hour before Marshall came out of the building. Then Sutter, at the door, motioned Matt to come in.

Was it his imagination, or was Sutter excited? Normally, the Swiss emigrant appeared calm and unruffled, but today his hands shook slightly and his eyes gleamed.

"Miller, I'm sorry to delay you like this, but the funds I expected haven't come yet. Why don't you go on back to Oregon, bring down another boatload of cattle, and I'll pay you for both of them when you come back?"

"I'm afraid I can't do that, Mr. Sutter. You see, my brother-in-law wanted me to use the money from the cattle sale to buy supplies. I'll wait."

Sutter blustered, "But I won't be here to entertain you, Mr. Miller. I have to go away for a few days."

When Matt didn't answer, but stared at him, waiting, Sutter said, "I must accompany Marshall up into the mountains, where he's doing some work for me."

"That's all right, sir. Since I can't be paid until you return, why don't I just mosey along with you? That way you can entertain me and check out Marshall's work at the same time."

Sutter plainly didn't want him along, and the next morning, when Matt joined them as they rode away from the fort, Marshall gave him a dirty look.

What has come over me? Matt wondered. Normally, he didn't meddle in the business of others. What had prompted him to follow Sutter and Marshall?

During the day's ride, he mingled with the servants, as well as with Marshall and Sutter, but no one divulged any reason for this journey to the American River. He'd probably have a long trip for nothing, but at least he could enjoy the scenery.

For the most part their trail followed the rims of deep, steep-sided canyons. When the cliffs proved too narrow for horseback riding and where a slip could mean a fall of a hundred feet, they moved to the high country. On the rare occasions when they rode beside the water, Matt marveled at the huge boulders in the streambeds.

On the second day, the travelers arrived at the sawmill site. Matt noticed several men beside the river's edge, scooping up pans of gravel and water, and suddenly he knew what had caused the excitement. Gold! Marshall had discovered the precious stuff, and he'd brought Sutter up to see it. Matt followed Sutter when he walked down to the American River, and his heart jumped when he saw the bright specks among the gravel.

Sutter reached for the pan a young man was swirling through the water and took a few golden chunks in his hand. He bit on one, and apparently forgetting Matt's presence, he said, "There's no doubt this is gold, but if you scooped up all the nuggets you see here, there wouldn't be much of it. Just forget it, Marshall, and go back to work. The same with you men; there's not enough gold here to make anyone rich. But do me a favor and don't say anything about what you've seen for at least six weeks, until this sawmill is finished."

There's enough gold to ruin you, Sutter, Matt thought. If news spread about the discovery of gold, thousands of people would travel here, put up a few flimsy shacks, dig holes all over the country, and drift away when the gold diminished. By that time, Sutter's sawmill site would be wrecked.

When Sutter prepared to leave the next morning, he looked questioningly at Matt, who'd made no effort to saddle his horse.

"I'm going to hang around a few days, if you don't mind. I panned for gold in the Rockies, when I traveled west, four years ago in forty-four. I didn't find anything then, so I thought I'd try my hand here."

"You're a fool, Miller; this gold isn't any good."

"Even if it isn't, I might as well put in my time up here rather than at the fort. If you want to get rid of me, pay for those cattle, and I'll be on my way."

Matt gave a few coins to one of the servants before they left. "Tell Sid Green that I'll be along in a few days."

Several hours passed before Matt again learned how to handle the pan properly; but by mid-afternoon, he'd gained back the necessary skill, dipping up a pan of soil, then submerging it in the water and stirring to break up the clods. When only the black sand containing the gold remained in his pan, he sifted it through his hands until he could extract the precious metal. At the end of the day, he'd panned a half cup of gold. His back and legs felt stiff from stooping, his feet were wet, and his hands bruised and bleeding from handling the icy water and gravel. After three days, he'd gleaned about fifty dollars' worth of gold and decided he'd had enough. He saddled up next morning and headed toward Sutter's Fort.

Pampering his sore hands and muscles, Matt rode slowly; he planned to take several days to reach the fort. When possible, he held to the river valley, but at times he climbed into the foothills. He liked the Sierras and toyed with the idea of moving to California permanently.

Matt wouldn't have been happy under Mexican rule, but now that the war was over and it seemed likely that the United States would gain control of the territory he might be content here. Matt ran his hands through his thick hair and shook his head wonderingly. Five years ago he'd operated a steamboat along the Ohio River, never dreaming that he'd ever leave, but in eighteen forty-four he'd brought his sister west over the Oregon Trail, and it seemed as though from that time wanderlust had tainted his blood. On the Ohio, he wouldn't have considered that he had an adventurous bone in his body, but already he'd had enough of Oregon.

Matt stirred restlessly in his saddle, realizing that he seemed always to be looking for something. He'd never gotten over losing Becky. For years his life had revolved around his sister, and when she'd married, his life lost its purpose. Not that he would deny her the happy life she had with Maurie and their child, but he missed her. Could he be lonely? *Admit it, you've always been lonely.*

A long time ago, he'd told Becky, "I only wish someone would love me the way you love Maurie." At thirty-eight, that wasn't likely, so he might as well stifle such thoughts.

A blast of cold air swirled snow flurries around him, and earlier than he'd intended, Matt hunted for a sheltered spot to make camp. He followed a deer path through the towering spruce trees until he came to a little cove.

Several uprooted trees marked the sheltered inlet, and it appeared that long ago an earthquake had tumbled part of the hill into the river. Hoping no quake would hit the region tonight, Matt rode to a small stream that fed the river, watered his horse, and filled a bucket with water for his own use.

Returning to higher ground, he unsaddled his horse and started a fire with the branches of a dead evergreen shrub. Then he pulled the whole shrub away from the loose gravel and dragged it closer to the fire.

As he turned to undo the pack from his saddle, his eyes detected bright color in the dirt on the roots of the shrub. "Gold," he whispered hoarsely and dropped to his knees beside the hole where the bush had been. His trembling hands reached to touch the earth that was littered with bright-yellow gold, in little pieces about the size of wheat grains.

Matt closed his eyes and swallowed convulsively. Surely this was a mirage! But when he opened his eyes, the gold was still there. "Gold!" he shouted. "Gold!" His hands dipped into the shiny nuggets that sifted easily through his fingers.

Working rapidly, Matt soon filled his skillet with the precious metal. When that hole was emptied, he ran to another fallen tree and jerked its roots from the ground.

More gold! This time, it came out in large chunks, and he hefted one piece that must have weighed over a pound.

What would this be worth in currency?

"I'm rich," Matt repeated over and over as he searched through the cove. Working by the light of the moon, Matt continued his labors throughout the night. Some of the fallen trees hid none of the ore at their roots, and when he could no longer scoop his riches by the handfuls, Matt grabbed a shovel he'd bought from Marshall and dug a tunnel between the trees where he'd found gold. One crevice was filled with a hard bluish clay, and when he used his knife to remove the clay, he discovered a small layer of nuggets.

While he searched, Matt's mind churned. He'd have to rush back to San Francisco and buy equipment to mine this whole hill. Why, he could be a millionaire in a few weeks! He'd buy Becky anything she wanted. She wouldn't have to work anymore. He'd buy Maurie the biggest ranch in Oregon. He'd be rich himself.

When Matt exhausted that supply of gold, he noticed his bleeding hands and suddenly became aware of his physical condition. He reeled like a drunken man, when he walked. Cold and hunger overwhelmed him. Where he'd started the fire last night, only blackened embers remained. His horse nickered, hungry no doubt, for where he was tied, the animal couldn't graze.

Matt collapsed on the ground and covered his face with his hands. "God, what am I doing?" he whispered. "The sight of this gold turned me into a madman." He hadn't had anything to eat since he'd left the sawmill, over twenty-four hours ago. He'd worked all night without any rest. Was this what gold did to a man?

"God," he prayed, "help me to overcome this temptation. Make me realize that life is more than riches. Yesterday, when I considered the lack in my life, I decided I was lonely. Much as I might think so, gold won't ease the loneliness. Guide me in the right way.

"This whole hill is probably full of gold. What should I do about it, Lord?"

Did he have any right to take the gold? Was this part of Sutter's holdings? Sutter didn't own the land at the sawmill, but did his grant from the Spanish extend this far? It wasn't likely that Sutter's title mentioned mineral rights, or he would have told the men at the sawmill that they couldn't hunt for gold on his property. Matt realized that legally he had as much right to this gold as anyone.

Matt sat for more than an hour, listening to God's message, then on unsteady feet, he went to his horse, untied the animal, and led him to a grassy spot at the edge of the cove. He rekindled the fire to prepare his breakfast, but all of his cooking utensils were full of gold. He emptied the skillet's contents into his saddlebags, fried some bacon, and mixed up a sourdough batter, which he cooked in bacon grease.

With his hunger satisfied, Matt stored all the gold in saddlebags and threw away his camping gear. When he arrived at Sutter's Fort, he didn't want it evident that he carried anything he hadn't had when he left the fort. He put the small packet of gold he'd gleaned from the American River in his pocket.

The sun was near the western horizon when, the next day, Matt arrived at the fort. He went first to his schooner, where he stored his gold in the cabin. After turning the horse into the corral, he walked up to Sutter's office. Sutter sat at his desk, hands folded over his stomach, staring out the window.

Matt knocked on the door, and Sutter jumped.

"Greetings, Mr. Miller. I didn't hear you." Sutter

reached into a drawer and handed Matt an envelope that contained a certificate of credit. "Present this to the American banking agent at Monterey, and you'll receive your money, sir. Sorry for the delay." He looked piercingly at Matt. "Did you find any gold?"

Matt took the small packet from his pocket. "I spent three days taking this from the riverbed. The way my back and legs felt at the end of that time, I decided panning gold wasn't for me."

"Miller, I hope you won't mention this when you return to San Francisco. Surely you can appreciate my position. If word circulates that gold has been found here, no matter how small the amount, hordes of people will flock to this area. I'd like to have some settlers move in here, but not gold seekers." He swept his arms wide. "A gold rush could ruin everything I've worked so long to build."

"You can be assured that your secret is safe with me. I know all too well that the desire for gold can turn a man into an animal."

As Matt's boat eased down the Sacramento River the next morning, he surveyed the scene before him. He felt sorry for Sutter. The gold strike wouldn't remain a secret, even if Matt never spread the word.

When they arrived at the San Francisco wharf, Matt said to Sid Green, "Tomorrow, I want you and one of the other men to take this certificate of credit to Monterey and exchange it for money. We'll not be able to go home until we buy Maurie's supplies."

Matt spent the night on the schooner, and the next morning, when all of his men had vacated the boat, he picked up the two saddlebags and headed uptown. In spite of the fact that Matt was a stocky, strong man, by the time he stopped before a wooden shack with the words

Spencer Shipping painted on the front, he breathed heavily from the load.

John Spencer, a bearded, tall, angular man of fifty-five, with reddish hair and brown eyes, rose from behind a littered desk to greet him.

"I'd decided you'd gone back to Oregon without stopping by. The trip took a long time."

Matt dropped the heavy saddlebags on the floor beside him, and commented, "Sutter was short of money as usual." He looked around casually. "All by yourself?"

"Yep. Not much doing this week. I'm going to the rancho tomorrow."

Matt went to the door and fastened the bar securely. "Let's keep this private, shall we?"

He lifted one bag and, trying to maintain his calm, unfastened the leather thongs on the flap to reveal the gleaming hoard of gold. As he did a thought flashed through his mind that he'd betrayed Sutter. But how long could it remain secret? Besides, he trusted John.

Spencer stared at him, astounded. "Man! Where'd you get this?"

"I picked that up on a hillside above the American River in about twelve hours' time. The other bag is full, too."

Spencer sat down weakly, as if his legs couldn't hold him any longer. He inserted his hand into the gold nuggets and sifted them through his fingers. "Tell me about it."

Matt described all that had happened. "It seems that when Marshall made one of his periodic tests of the millrace, by leaving the sluice gates open all night to allow the water to cascade through, the next morning he noticed tiny yellow specks at the bottom of the millrace. After he made a few simple tests, he knew he'd found gold and he rushed to tell Sutter."

"Was Sutter excited over it?"

"Nope. He made light of the discovery, trying to convince his men that the gold wasn't worth anything. I wasn't so sure, and since I had to wait on Sutter, I tried my hand at panning."

Matt hurriedly completed the tale of his discovery, and Spencer exclaimed, "Why, Matt, you must have close to a half million dollars here!"

"That's the way I figure it. And the more of that gold I scooped up, the more I acted like a madman, crazy to get more and more. When I finally realized how I'd been carrying on, it dawned on me what a curse gold can be. I remembered what the Bible said about the love of money being the root of all evil, and I sat for an hour allowing God to deal with what had happened to me."

"If anyone learns how much gold you found in one day, this country will become a beehive. It will be the ruination of our way of life."

"I don't intend to tell anyone else. I wouldn't have told you, if I didn't need advice on what to do with this."

"But *can* it remain a secret?"

"I don't think so. I believe that country is thick with gold. I watched the riverbed as I rode back to Sutter's, and I saw gold gleaming all along the way."

"It must have been a great temptation not to stay there and scoop up all you could find."

"At first I was frantic. I wanted to mine that whole hill, become a millionaire. In my mind, I spent money like King Midas. But I've had time to think about it on the way downriver these past five days. One day of gold fever was enough to cure me. I'm going to invest this and make money by doing what I like to do, not digging in the ground like a gopher. I believe a man is happier if he makes his living by the sweat of his brow."

"This is enough to buy a good rancho," Spencer said.

"No ranching for me, John. I've never been satisfied since I left my steamboat on the Ohio River. If the news of this gold strike leaks out, in a few months, there'll be a big demand for transportation up the Sacramento River to the fields. If I hurry, I can have a steamboat ready to handle that traffic."

"Yes, I was thinking the same thing. Spencer Shipping should have lots of mining equipment ready, and you could haul that and other supplies for us. Sounds to me as if the most common commodity in this area within a year could be gold. Any merchant who has a big supply of goods will help provision people and make money, too."

"Advise me, John. What should I do?"

"Turn this gold into credit as soon as possible. I'd say the best place to do that is on the East Coast."

"But you're talking about a year's travel. By the time I'd go east and back, the gold rush would be over."

"I didn't mean a trip around the Horn. The fastest way to travel to the States now is to go by water to Panama, cross land there, and pick up another ship on the Caribbean side and travel north. That can be done in six weeks, on a route started during the war. We have a boat leaving for Panama in a few days." He glanced at a new eighteen forty-eight calendar, hanging behind the desk. "Let's see, this is February twelfth. If you're lucky, you could be in Boston near the first of April."

"I hate to leave without seeing my sister and her husband."

"Send word to them by Green. He can take the schooner home without you. You need to move fast."

"Why did you say Boston? I could exchange this gold for credit in places nearer than that."

Spencer's lips parted in a smile behind his reddish

beard. "Two reasons. First, the boat you'll find in the Caribbean will be a Spencer boat bound for New England. The other reason, I want you to take a message to my family in Boston to send loads of supplies to me."

"Can those come by Panama?"

"No, they'll have to be shipped around the Horn, which could take six months, but I don't think there'll be a big demand before then. I hope by that time I will have turned this business over to someone else and retired to the rancho. I'll especially need to be there now, to keep it from being overrun by gold seekers."

"Who's going to take over? Your brother?" Matt remembered that John's brother owned Spencer Shipping.

"My brother has died, but his daughter and her husband should be coming to operate this end of the business Another son-in-law will supervise the company in Boston. Could work out well, if the two men are good managers. I'll be glad to have some of my relations on this side of the continent, and Unity was always my favorite niece."

Spencer drew a daguerreotype portrait from a drawer. "These are my nieces. Unity is the one that's coming to California. She's the younger," he said, pointing to one of the girls, "but she must be around twenty-five now."

A faint look of disgust crossed the man's features. "Though he was a God-fearing man, in one way my brother wasn't wise. He used his daughters as pawns to improve his shipping business. Since he didn't have any sons to carry on, he manipulated his daughters' marriages to benefit himself. Unity is married to Samuel Whitley, whose family has been in the shipping industry since the early seventeen hundreds. I just hope he makes her a good husband."

John pushed aside the papers in his safe, and they

wedged the two bags of nuggets inside. The next morning Matt bought a barrel in which to store the gold and addressed it to himself, in care of Spencer Shipping in Boston, where he'd claim it upon his arrival.

Matt waited anxiously for Sid Green's return, wanting to see his friend started northward with the schooner before he sailed. Meanwhile he labored long over a letter to Becky and her husband.

Dear Sister and Maurie:

I hardly know how to explain my sudden departure for the East. While I waited for Sutter to produce the money for your cattle, I came into some riches. Actually, I struck gold, as incredible as that sounds, lots of gold, and I'm going East to convert it into credit. I think the rate of exchange is better there, and if anyone here would know the amount of gold I found, it would start an instant rush for Sutter's ranch. The news is bound to get out, but I don't want to be the one responsible for spreading it.

While I'm in the East, I'm going to buy an engine for a steamboat. The time has come, I think, to start the business that I've talked about, and I'll be operating here in the Sacramento River. This country is bound to grow, and I want to grow with it.

Sid Green had known Matt a long time and probably knew he wouldn't get any information out of him, so he didn't ask any questions, but he did look puzzled when he learned Matt wasn't returning to Oregon. Instead of commenting on his employer's uncharacteristic behavior, he said, "The treaty has been signed to end the war between the United States and Mexico. California belongs to the United States now."

This news prompted a general rejoicing among the inhabitants of the little port, for several of its eight hundred residents were Americans, and it further strengthened Matt's desire to live in California.

Handing Green a bag of coins, Matt ordered, "Pay the men when you arrive in Oregon City. After you take this letter to Maurie, spend several months at home, then bring the schooner back to San Francisco and wait until I return. I hope to be here by the first of June."

"What're your plans, Matt?"

"I'm going to resettle here and start running a boat on the Sacramento. Now that California is a part of the United States, I figure the region will grow rapidly. If you want to continue to work with me, come prepared to stay when you bring the schooner down in June."

Sid glanced around moodily. "I don't know if that'd suit me, but I'll think about it."

On the day of departure, John Spencer accompanied Matt to the dock. Matt glanced through the list of goods that Spencer was ordering. "You'll need two or three ships to bring all of these, John."

Spencer nodded agreement. "I know I'm gambling, and if we don't have a stampede, I'm in trouble, but whether or not there's much gold, as soon as the news is out, people will pour in. I've ordered volumes of foodstuffs and clothing, as well as mining equipment and several loads of lumber."

"Even if there isn't a gold rush, I figure this country will build up, now that Americans are in control."

"Bound to." John sealed the list in an envelope addressed to *Isaac Smith, Spencer Shipping, Boston, Massachusetts*.

"That's the man who'll be in charge of buying on that end, so see him as soon as you arrive in Boston. He'll also be able to advise you about where to exchange your gold."

"You'd better come along, John. It's been a long time since you've been to the States."

"Ten years. But I don't want to return. California is home now."

Spencer left the deck of the ship and waved to Matt as the vessel loosed its mooring and slipped down San Francisco Bay toward the Pacific.

3

*N*ow that she'd made the decision to go to California, Unity wanted to discuss Levi's future with Deborah. As she started downstairs, she heard a knock on the front door and since Margaret was away from home, the butler approached Unity.

"There's a Lieutenant Calvin Swisher and wife to visit Mr. Smith."

"Perhaps I'd better see them first."

Swisher, a tall, straight man, rose as she entered the drawing room.

"Mr. Smith is quite ill, but I'm his sister-in-law. If there's a business matter, perhaps I can take care of it."

Swisher indicated the plump woman with graying hair, seated beside him. "This is Loretta, my wife. We wanted to talk with Mr. Smith about California. We understand he's been there. Now that the war with Mexico has ended, I'm being transferred to the military garrison at Monterey. I want to take Loretta with me, but I'd like to know about the living conditions and how we should travel."

God, is this the answer to one of my problems?

"Will you be seated and have some refreshment while I ask Isaac if he'll see you? I'll send the maid in with some tea and cakes."

Isaac had just awakened from a nap, and he seemed interested in talking with the Swishers. As Unity left the room to summon their guests, he said, "This may be an opportunity for you to travel to California in the company of a woman."

"I had the same thought. I'll bring them up to see you."

"My main concern is for my wife, sir," Swisher said to Isaac, after they'd briefly discussed California's culture and terrain. "What kind of conditions should she expect? Will there be any suitable company for her?"

"It's a crude land, and she won't have many comforts except what you take along. However, now that the United States has gained control over it, I'm sure it won't be long until many citizens will travel out there. As for company. . . ." he gasped for breath and nodded to Unity.

"I'm planning to leave for California soon," she said. "My husband and I were supposed to go there to manage the family's shipping business, but since his death and Isaac's illness, there hasn't been anyone to go. I'm planning to join my uncle, John Spencer, at San Francisco. I would be pleased to have your wife's company as I travel."

Relief was mirrored on the faces of both Swishers. "My sailing orders are for two weeks from now. Would it be convenient for you to travel that soon? I'm to take passage to Panama, cross overland, and go by ship up the Pacific Coast." He turned to Isaac. "Is that feasible, sir?"

Isaac nodded. "A hard trip, but possible, I understand,

although I've not traveled that route. It's much faster than going around the Horn."

A tap on the door interrupted them, and excusing herself, Unity opened to the butler, who said softly, "A gentleman to see Mr. Isaac."

"I'll see him first."

Unity entered the drawing room to be greeted by a brawny, dark-complexioned man. Although he was of medium height, this man radiated strength from every muscle of his well-developed body. "I'm Matt Miller," he introduced himself. "I'm newly arrived from California and I have a letter for Isaac Smith, but the butler says he's ill."

"Yes, he is. If it's a matter of business, I might help you."

"Are you Smith's wife?"

"No, his sister-in-law."

"Then you must be Unity Whitley," he said.

"Yes, but how did you know?"

He smiled slightly. "I'm a friend of your uncle John, and he showed me a picture of you before I left. He mentioned that you and your husband would be coming to California."

"My husband drowned several months ago. I am, however, leaving for California in a few weeks, and I'll be pleased to hear news of the area. Won't you sit down?"

"Maybe you should read this letter. It's rather urgent." He waited while she read the missive and glanced through the lists of items John Spencer had ordered.

"A very strange tale, Mr. Miller. A gold strike."

"Gold has been found, all right, and very likely when the news spreads, there will be a stampede of would-be miners to the region. But I'd advise you to avoid any mention of the gold outside the family. Let the news come from an official source.

"I'm going to be opening a steamboat line in the area, and John wants all those items so I can transport them to the gold fields if a rush is on."

"How many people are there in San Francisco?"

"About eight hundred, I'd judge."

"But if there isn't a rush of people to the area, looks as if Spencer Shipping will be stuck with lots of supplies."

"I see you know your business, ma'am," Matt agreed in surprise. "John knows it's a gamble, but as long as it takes to ship supplies around the Horn, they may be needed by the time these goods arrive in California."

"Since Isaac isn't able to handle this, I'll have to take over, Mr. Miller. Before you go, I'd like to ask you some questions about the journey to California. I'll be traveling with an army officer and his wife."

"The trip around the Horn isn't so difficult, but it's long and tedious, I've heard."

"We aren't going around the Horn. We plan to take the Panama route."

"If I may advise you, ma'am, I'd say that's a mistake. I came that way myself; it was a miserable trip."

"How do you plan to return?"

"The same way I came. I'm in a hurry."

"It must not be too bad, if you're willing to return that way. I understand that by going through Panama, we can reach California in approximately two months. Frankly, I have no desire for a long ocean voyage. I went with my father several times to the Caribbean Islands, and I grew weary of the lack of activity aboard ship. What's so bad about Panama?"

"The mosquitoes and fleas attack you. There isn't any

decent place to sleep. You'll have to travel over twenty miles on muleback—or walk. It's a hard trip."

"I'll make it."

"Then it might be well for you to dose yourself with quinine before you leave and take plenty of medicine along. I was down with a fever for several days on the sea voyage from Panama to Boston."

"Thank you for delivering the message. If you have time, perhaps you can stop by our warehouse near the harbor. I'll probably have questions about these items." She tapped the list John had sent.

"And Mr. Miller," she said as Matt stood, "we plan to leave in two weeks' time. Perhaps I shouldn't ask this, but I'm presuming on your friendship with Uncle John. I'd appreciate it very much if you'd travel back to California when I do."

Their eyes held for a long minute, and Unity wondered why she so quickly trusted this man. True, he was John Spencer's friend, but none of her uncle's other friends had caused her heart to behave in this unseemly manner.

"If I can conclude my business by then, I'll be happy to accompany you, ma'am."

After Matt's departure, Unity glanced over the long list of items John wanted. Buying these goods would take many hours, but Unity welcomed the opportunity to keep busy. That would give her something to think about besides the fact that she must leave Levi behind when she set sail for California.

Unity knelt beside the cradle and touched Levi lightly on the face. How could she possibly leave him? But wouldn't it be more difficult to see him every day and not be allowed to mother him?

"My son," she whispered, "it isn't that I don't love you,

but I'm doing what I think best. If there were a better way. . . ."

The boy opened his eyes, and giving Unity a sleepy smile, he reached a hand to grasp the ribbons of her bonnet. She wondered sometimes how she could love the child with such intensity when he looked so much like his father. The boy had inherited her reddish-brown hair, but otherwise his features mirrored Samuel's. She laid her finger on the cleft in his chin, the most obvious trait in his small face that marked the child as a Whitley.

God, she prayed silently, *You know I don't want to make the wrong decision.* For days now fear that Margaret would mistreat the boy had haunted Unity. If Isaac recovered, there would be no cause for alarm, for he'd make a good father, but so far her brother-in-law's health hadn't improved. *Keep my son and guide his path.*

Unity lifted the boy from his cradle and snuggled him in her arms. She peered again into his face, trying to memorize every detail of his features to carry with her. She did have a small daguerreotype, taken two months ago, but even in that short time he'd changed a great deal.

The door into the nursery opened, and Margaret posed there, displeasure on her face. Unity gave her baby one final hug, kissed him, and laid him tenderly in the cradle. She rose from her knees and faced her sister.

"If it weren't for Isaac's health, I'd take him with me. With Levi in California, it isn't likely the Whitleys would ever find him."

"You made a bargain, remember?" Margaret answered quietly.

"And I'm keeping my part of the bargain, even though *you* didn't keep *yours.*"

Margaret turned, saying over her shoulder, "The Swishers are waiting for you downstairs."

Unity took another long look at Levi before she left the room. Her trunks had already been sent to the wharf, and she'd made her good-byes to Isaac, but she went to Deborah's room.

Deborah folded Unity in a tight embrace. "I wish I could go with you, Miss Unity."

"I wish so, too. If it weren't for Levi, I'd have taken you, but I'll feel more at ease if you're here to watch over him."

"Don't worry about the little tyke. I'll keep Miss Margaret in line."

Before she followed the Swishers into the coach, Unity turned for one last look at the sprawling, two-storied frame house. She'd been born here; her marriage had taken place in the drawing room. Was she leaving it for the last time? Somehow she felt that she was, and with effort she forced back tears that were near the surface.

Matt paced the deck of the clipper *Panama*, eager to start his return journey. He'd stayed in Boston for two weeks, and they'd been busy days, for in addition to taking care of his own business, he had supervised the loading of John Spencer's supplies. Yesterday Matt had watched three Spencer vessels sail for California, and he was eager to follow them.

The idea that he was a rich man had slowly infiltrated Matt's brain, and it scared him. He didn't want riches to ruin him, as he'd seen it do to other men. But how could he handle the fact that in one day's time he'd picked up gold amounting to a half million dollars? He'd deposited most of the money gained from the gold in a Boston bank, but he carried over twenty thousand dollars in a belt around his waist, and it felt as heavy as lead.

The lumber to build his boat and the steam engine to operate it were on one of the Spencer ships sailing around the Horn, but his feet rested on a crate containing a smaller engine that he was taking with him. With this engine on his schooner, he could start a transportation service immediately.

Matt's large amount of gold had occasioned much curiosity at the assayer's office, but he had refused to divulge where he'd found it. Before long news of California's gold would spread worldwide, but he didn't want to be the one to circulate the story that would ruin Sutter's Eden.

Last week a short article had appeared in a Boston newspaper.

Gold in California? Or Is It a Hoax?

The soldiers interviewed had not seen the gold themselves, but they'd heard the news before they started eastward. However, it was reported that gold was being picked up from the streams, and the soldiers said that over half the population of the village of San Francisco had taken off for the mountains, several days' travel away. Many soldiers delayed their homecoming and went to investigate the story for themselves. But, folks, I wouldn't buy my shovel yet.

A few more stories like that, and Matt knew gold seekers from the States would pour into California. Could he arrive there before the rush started?

His attention was drawn to the coach pulling up at the dock, and he saw a man in uniform handing down two women. This would be the Swishers, who were traveling with Unity Whitley. Matt watched Unity's tall, graceful figure as she boarded the ship, and he bowed as she reached him.

"Good morning, Mrs. Whitley."

"Good morning, Mr. Miller." She looked at him carefully. "Will you address me as *Miss Spencer* from now on? Even though I'm a widow, I've taken back my maiden name. Since I'm going to be managing Spencer Shipping, it seemed best that way."

He nodded. "Your three ships are on the way now, ma'am. Left yesterday."

"Judging by that article in the paper this week, it seems as though there may be a need for all those supplies."

She passed into the aft cabin that she would share with Loretta Swisher, and within the hour, the crew had set the sails, untied the ship from the dock, and moved the boat seaward. Matt noted only three other passengers besides Unity, the Swishers, and himself. *It should be a fairly pleasant voyage,* he thought.

When she returned to the deck, Unity had removed her bonnet. She leaned against the rail, her eyes focused on the town until the ship cleared the bay and reached the open sea. Matt noticed that her eyes were moist when she turned toward her cabin.

The meals were to be served in the wardroom where the passengers were invited to sit with the captain. Their first meal, in late afternoon, would be expected to last them until tomorrow morning. Lieutenant Swisher was a taciturn man who devoted most of his time to eating, but Loretta Swisher had an easy way of talking. She directed most of her remarks to Captain Turner, who spoke at length about his many years of service in the China trade. Matt never had a great deal to say to strangers, and Unity was equally silent.

"Make the most of this meal, folks," Captain Turner announced. "After a few days, the fresh foods will be gone, and we'll be down to salt pork and beans. We do, however, have lots of lemons and cider, which we want you to consume in great quantities, to prevent scurvy."

After the supper hour Matt walked back and forth on the deck, content to be underway again. He liked the feel of the deck under his feet, and he lifted his head and savored the salty, tangy spray from the waves. The rigging snapped as the sails billowed above his head. The ship's course led southwest, and the sun hovered on the horizon, suspended in space, it seemed, while saffron and crimson rays darted across the sky.

" 'They that go down to the sea in ships, that do business in great waters; These see the works of the Lord, and his wonders in the deep,' " Unity's voice, quoting the psalm, sounded at his elbow.

Matt turned toward her with his slow smile.

"Not hard to believe in the Lord when you see a sight like that. Sunset is always my favorite time on the water."

"That sky promises good weather tomorrow, I guess."

"Sure does, and the more good weather we have, the faster we'll travel. I'm eager to get home."

Two sea gulls flew over, and their raucous cries pierced the calmness of the scene as the *Panama* rose slowly on the slight swell of water. The gentle movement of the ship was pleasant, yet a chill tinged the breeze, and Unity sat on a pile of rope in the protection of the cabin.

"How long has California been your home, Mr. Miller?"

"It never has been. I've lived in Oregon for the past four years; before that I operated a boat on the Ohio River for several years. I'm going to settle in California now."

"So, like the Spencers, you're gambling your future on a gold rush."

"I suppose so."

"Don't you have any inclination to search for more gold? Uncle John said in his letter that you'd made a big strike."

He stared at her, openmouthed. He hadn't known John had written that. The fewer people who knew he was rich, the happier he'd be. "I found enough to know that I don't want any more prospecting, ma'am. Besides, only a little vision is needed to know that the ones who accumulate riches in this gold rush will be those who have something to sell. I'll make plenty of money, Miss Spencer, but it will be in honest toil."

"Honesty means a great deal to you?"

"Absolutely."

After Unity went to her cabin, Matt stood by the rail while darkness settled around him. He'd never known a woman like Unity Spencer. In the days they'd worked together, buying supplies for the California trade, he'd learned to admire her business acumen. She had a keenness of mind he'd not seen in another of her sex. Although admitting that his knowledge of females was scant, he knew an unusual one when he saw her.

Matt wondered about Unity's husband. If she mourned him, she did a good job of hiding it. True, he hadn't seen her smile until this evening, when they'd talked together, and she had seemed on the verge of tears when the ship had departed from the harbor. So maybe she felt sorrow over losing her husband after all. Matt surprised himself by hoping that she wouldn't mourn him very long.

For the next few days, the passengers saw little of one another; all succumbed to seasickness and spent most of the time in their cabins. Matt hated the nauseous feeling that swept over him hour after hour, and he longed to leave the ocean and return to placid rivers. His journeys from Oregon to California hadn't caused any seasickness, because he'd hugged the coast as much as possible.

Several days after that the *Panama* sailed southwesterly without incident. Occasionally the passengers glimpsed the nearby coastline. The farther south they traveled, the warmer the weather became, and the sea breeze lost most of its crispness. Loretta and Unity spent the daylight hours on deck to escape their sweltering cabin. Loretta devoted her time to knitting, and sometimes Unity read, but often she sat with folded hands, waiting.

After a week of calm weather, the sunrise appeared as glowing as the sunsets had been, and Matt figured their peaceful journey was threatened. When Unity stopped beside him, he said, "You were quoting Psalm One Hundred and Seven to me a few days ago. Remember some of the other verses?" he asked her with a smile.

"No, I don't," she said, but she went to her cabin and returned with a Bible. " 'For he commandeth, and raiseth the stormy wind,' " she read, " 'which lifteth up the waves thereof. They mount up to the heaven, they go down again to the depths: their soul is melted because of trouble. They reel to and fro, and stagger like a drunken man, and are at their wit's end.' "

"I always thought that David wrote all of the Psalms, but the man who penned those lines had to be a sailor. I expect we'll be experiencing all of that before another twenty-four hours ends."

"Perhaps," Unity said calmly, "but don't forget the following verses, 'Then they cry unto the Lord in their trouble, and he bringeth them out of their distresses. He maketh the storm a calm, so that the waves thereof are still. Then are they glad because they be quiet; so he bringeth them unto their desired haven.' "

When she returned to her cabin, Unity pondered the psalm, not so much thinking of the approaching storm, but hoping that the words were a portent of peace for her personal future.

That afternoon the *Panama* encountered a stiff breeze, which turned into a strong wind in a few hours. When dark clouds swirled across the skies, the captain ordered his men to furl the sails so they could wait out the storm. Soon cold rain hammered the deck, and the passengers sought shelter. Lieutenant Swisher went into the captain's cabin with the women, while the captain ordered the other travelers below deck.

Matt didn't relish the idea of being down under, if the ship sank, so he elected to stay on deck, wryly admitting to himself that under those circumstances it wouldn't matter where he was. Observing the whirling, spinning waves, he wondered if he'd ever see California again.

The storm broke in earnest, with the wind screaming through the yards. Sails ripped as the white-capped sea tilted and tossed the ship. Foaming water splashed over the port side and swirled around Matt's feet, and he noticed that the helmsman had roped himself to his post.

Captain Turner, holding on a line, slid by Matt's covert. "Miller, you should be below, but if you're crazy enough to stay up here, lend a hand. One of my men didn't lash down some cargo well, and it's about to smash up the deck. He needs help." He pointed to a sailor who was doggedly trying to push a large wooden box nearer the gunwale. Just as he seemed successful, a crest of water broke over the rail and sent the box and seaman skidding amidships. Cargo littered the deck about him.

Matt carefully waded toward the man, and together, after what seemed like hours, they finally forced the first box into place. As he sought some line to tie it down with, Unity suddenly appeared at Matt's side, carrying a bundle of the sturdy rope.

With each wave that broke across the deck, Matt had thought the ship was doomed. Yet now, as he feared for Unity's safety, he exulted in her courage.

Even the waves that overwhelmed her deck could not

halt the *Panama*. When one of the seamen, swept off his feet by a wave, tumbled into the ocean, Matt yelled to Unity, "Take care! Don't go near the rail," but if she heard him, she didn't heed his advice, only helping pull the line taut around another box they'd forced into place. Every few seconds the ship rose on a mountain of water, only to drop immediately into a foaming pit.

As they wrapped the last of the line around the final barrel, Matt realized his feet and hands had lost all feeling. When he thought he couldn't endure another moment of the storm, the seas calmed perceptibly, and like a weary woman, the *Panama* slowed to a crawl over the water. Matt dropped to the deck, his head on his arms, but he soon roused and looked for Unity. She had collapsed on her back, near him, and he crawled to her. The wet cloak was molded to her body, and reddish hair hung in tatters around her face and shoulders.

"Are you all right, ma'am?"

She blinked and nodded.

"Shouldn't you change into dry garments?"

"I couldn't move now if my life depended on it. Anyway, I doubt if there's anything dry on this ship."

Too tired to argue, Matt sprawled on the deck beside her. They must have slept for an hour before Captain Turner awakened them. The evening sun shone in their faces as they sat up groggily to survey the damage around them.

Sailors were already aloft, mending the sails and rigging. Matt crawled across the slippery deck to the crate holding his steam engine and felt thankful to find it undamaged. When they congregated on the deck to hear Captain Spencer read a brief memorial service for the seamen who'd been lost, Matt breathed a prayer of thanks that the loss of life hadn't been great.

Two weeks later the *Panama* moved serenely into the

harbor of Chagres, in Panama. The jungle reached the water's edge, and the passengers couldn't see the village, but on top of the cliff they saw an imposing stone castle.

"There's a hotel of sorts at Chagres, and I'd suggest you rest there a few days before you start your land journey," Captain Turner told them. "I'll arrange for your passage overland as part of the fare you paid in Boston. The journey from here to Panama City, the seaport on the Pacific, will take at least a week."

"I think two nights here will be enough for me," Matt said. "How about the rest of you?"

When the other passengers nodded assent, Turner said, "For seven of you and your baggage, I'll arrange for three boats. I'll meet you at the hotel in a couple of days to start you on your journey."

"I've already had about all of this village I want," Unity said to Matt the next morning, when they met at breakfast. The fat pork and bread had been served on the veranda of the hotel, and while Unity tried to force the food down her throat, she looked with disfavor on the muddy little village of bamboo-pole houses with thatched roofs. Though she had bathed before leaving the room, her skin already felt hot and sticky.

Matt nodded agreement as he swigged the black, strongly brewed coffee, but he said, "I warned you."

"I doubt the voyage around the Horn would have been any more comfortable."

"Maybe not," Matt said, but he sounded unconvinced. "I had hoped to move on today, but I think the Swishers are pretty much exhausted, so perhaps it's just as well to rest longer. The trip to the Pacific will tax everyone's strength."

Becoming aware of some excitement along the river, Matt and Unity hurried that way. A canoe, poled by two men, moved quickly toward the bank.

"Any ships in the harbor?" one of them called in English, and when the natives gesticulated and jabbered in Spanish, Matt answered, "One, at least. The *Panama* arrived yesterday."

"We want to book passage northward." The man's voice was loud, and he moved with quick, jerky steps as he tied up the boat. He motioned Matt to one side, and Matt tucked his hand under Unity's elbow, so she would follow him.

"Buddy, are you and your wife headed for California?"

With a slight grin in Unity's direction, Matt nodded.

The stranger took a leather bag from his trousers, untied it with trembling fingers, and spread it wide before Matt. "I'm going to let you in on some great news. Look at this. What do you think it is?"

Glancing at the gleaming gravel in the bag, Matt *knew* what it was. Hadn't he scooped it up by the handfuls not many months ago? But the man didn't wait for his answer.

"It's gold, buddy, gold! I jumped ship in San Francisco, three months ago, and headed into the mountains. In a month my friend and I picked up enough gold to make us rich. Gold is thicker than fleas up there."

"Why did you leave, if gold is that plentiful?"

"I'm going home to tell my brothers about this before the news is widespread. Before we left, people were pouring into the gold fields from Oregon and Mexico—even a bunch of Chinese from the Sandwich Islands. If I can tell my brothers before everyone on the East Coast hears, we can hurry out there, and all of us will be rich. We want to take a boat out of here as soon as possible."

"Captain Turner is the man to see. Look for him in the hotel."

After he rushed away, Unity said, "So it's started already!"

"Yes, and I figure the storm we endured on the *Panama* will be calm compared to the one this gold will cause. But no need to worry about that until we arrive in California. Do you feel up to a trip to the castle?"

Unity looked upward to the huge structure towering above them. Then she glanced down at the high-heeled shoes she wore.

"Why not? After I change into some walking boots."

Even with Matt's assistance, Unity's strength faltered before they reached the castle. In places jungle grass covered the rocky path, and Matt had to clear it often with a machete. Several times they stopped to rest, once under a coconut tree, where Matt knocked two of the fruit down and broke their shells. Matt and Unity quenched their thirst on the cool liquid. Later they paused beside an orange tree, and although the fruit had a bitter taste, the tart liquid strengthened them.

When they finally stood on the castle's rampart and viewed the broad expanse of the Caribbean Sea, they agreed it had been worth the strenuous climb.

"Oh, Matt," Unity breathed. "Can you believe such beauty?"

"When I passed through here in March, I was told that the view from this mountain was amazing. Now I believe it."

"Look at those gentle waves splashing on the beach. I'd like to spend the day wading in that surf. The tide here is so much gentler than it is along the New England coast. For the past year it seems as if life has battered me the way the storm lashed and tossed the *Panama*. That scene almost makes me believe that I've reached the lull in the storm."

"Yes, but after a lull, doesn't the storm often beat harder?"

Unity laughed at him. "Joy killer! Won't you even allow me to imagine a calm future?" She grabbed his hand. "But I won't let you spoil my day. Let's explore this castle."

Much of the interior lay in ruins, but they spent hours going from one massive room to another. Remains of human habitation were evident in some of the rooms, and Unity said, "I can almost imagine this place when pirates lived here. Just think of the big parties they must have thrown, the executions of their enemies, and a lookout on the tower signaling that another ship they could plunder was heading toward shore."

"Be glad they aren't here, Unity, or *we* might be the enemies who would have to walk the plank."

Thoughts of pirates brought the Whitleys to mind, and suddenly Unity lost interest in the castle.

They sat on the rampart, eating the cheese and bread Matt had brought from the village and more of the oranges he'd stored in his pockets. Before leaving, they took one last look at the expansive sea below.

Dusk was falling when Matt and Unity reached the hotel, and they sat with the Swishers during the unpalatable evening meal. Flies crawled over the food, and mosquitoes swarmed around their heads. Outside, pigs and dogs quarreled over the table scraps, but Unity could ignore it all because of the pleasant day they'd spent.

When they finished eating, Matt said, "Thanks for your company today, Unity."

She laid her hand in his. "And thank you. This pleasant day will bolster me for the difficult journey ahead. Good night, Matt."

As Unity undressed in the darkness, to thwart any further influx of mosquitoes, she realized that sometime during the day, she and Matt had passed to a first-name basis. And why not? This day with him had provided her with more pleasant memories than she'd had from several months with Samuel Whitley. Covering her head with the thin blanket, she lamented, "Why couldn't I have met him before Samuel Whitley came into my life?"

At the river's edge three flat-bottomed boats, called bongos, awaited the travelers. The wide rear section of two of the boats had been covered with canvas, under which lay benches. Several natives, naked to the waist and holding long poles, manned the front of the boats. The baggage, along with sacks of rice, dried pork, and bundles of sugar cane, were piled on the third boat.

Matt and Unity rode with the Swishers, and the remaining travelers occupied the other boat. Soon they left Chagres behind and entered walls of green that marked the beginning of the jungle. For the most part, the river remained shallow and narrow and slow moving, but in some places it widened and water surged around them in white-capped rapids.

Vines covered many of the slender palm trees, and numerous wide-leaved bushes intertwined their branches with giant plants. Bright flowers of red, yellow, and purple swarmed over the green foliage. To get relief from the warm and moist air Unity occasionally trailed her hand through the warm water, until one of the boatmen saw what she was doing and with excited gestures passed a message that she shouldn't dangle her fingers in the water. Matt pointed toward the bank. Once she saw the rough backs of several crocodiles, Unity kept her hands in the boat.

Monkeys squalled from the trees, and bright-plumaged birds flitted through the branches, calling to one another in shrill voices that startled the passengers.

"Are those parrots?" Loretta asked.

Her husband nodded. "Some are. They can be taught to talk, if you want one," her husband said with a rare touch of humor.

"No, thank you! I'd rather *you'd* talk to me a little more."

At the village of Gatun, where they had to spend the night, Unity took one look at the vermin-infested cane mats inside the building and commented, "I'll be more comfortable sleeping outside." When Loretta agreed with her, they decided to use the canvas hammocks Captain Turner had provided for them. The mosquitoes feasted on them throughout the night, but at least they breathed fresh air.

Scratching furiously at a mosquito bite, Unity stirred in the hammock and drifted back to sleep. Ocean waves broke around her, and she clutched Levi in her arms. "No, no," she shouted as the waves dashed at her feet. She had to protect her boy. Looking around for a means of escape, she saw that the water surrounded her. She was trapped. "Levi! Levi!" she muttered. "I love you. I'll take care of you."

As she wiped the water from her face she realized her arms were empty. Instead Matt Miller stood beside her. "Unity, wake up. You'll have to come inside the hut."

Torrential rain fell around them. No wonder she'd dreamed water surrounded her. Loretta and Calvin already crouched in the crowded hut, when she and Matt entered. A candle stuck in a can revealed several natives and a bevy of dogs occupying the center of the room, with the travelers clustered around them. The thatched roof provided scant protection from the downpour; Unity felt a mist on her face.

"What time is it?" she whispered to Matt.

"Four o'clock."

"Does this mean we won't be traveling today?"

"The sun will probably be shining by daylight, but we'll have these sudden showers the rest of the trip, so keep your raincoat handy. And don't forget to dose yourself with quinine."

Unity ran her hand across the back of her neck to relieve the crawling sensation of her flesh.

"Fleas," Matt said.

"What?"

"Fleas are crawling on you. That's the reason your neck itches."

"Gracious! Will I ever be clean again?"

"Not for several days at any rate. I still think you should have gone around the Horn."

"Mr. Miller, you have some archaic ideas about women. We're not weaklings. I'll wager Loretta and I will stand this trip as well as the rest of you."

Unity suspected that she'd hit a sore point with Matt, although his next statement took no notice of her comment. "What was your husband's name?" he questioned.

"*Samuel. Samuel Whitley.* Why do you ask?"

"Curiosity, I guess."

That's the only answer he gave her, but she didn't think it was the correct one, for Matt Miller didn't strike her as a particularly curious man.

Intermittent downpours and the humid rays of the tropical sun besieged their next day of travel, but it brought them to the village of Gorgona. Early the next morning, climbing on mules, they began the last lap of their journey toward the Pacific. Before noon, the narrow, winding trail, with its mountains, steep cliffs, streams, and steaming jungles, had sapped Unity's strength.

"We're traveling along the old route that the Spanish used to ship their gold and silver from Peru to Spain," Calvin told them during a rest stop.

"I wish they'd used some of the gold to smooth out this trail. Every muscle in my body is complaining," Loretta said.

After lunch the mules picked their way, single file, over a narrow, stony jungle trail. Forests of vine-covered palms often plunged them into darkness, and the mules stumbled over fallen trees in their path. The animals, struggling to keep their footing in the swollen streams, splashed the brackish liquid over their riders.

In spite of her discomfort, Unity appreciated the beauty around her. Even when the way seemed the hardest, the flowers glowed with intense beauty, and hundreds of colorful birds flitted through the forest.

Isn't it the same way with life? she pondered. *When it seems the most difficult, God always provides a ray of light.* Matt Miller had furnished the brightness on this otherwise-miserable trip. His companionship had eased the fact that she was traveling farther and farther from her son.

Inwardly Unity voiced the words of the Apostle, "I can do all things through Christ which strengtheneth me." How grateful she felt that Christ had sent Matt to help her during this crucial time.

To Loretta, who rode beside her for a few miles when the trail widened, Unity said, "Don't you feel wonderful, experiencing this? Not many women would have the courage to undertake such a journey."

With a smile in her voice, Loretta said, "Right now, I don't think it's so wonderful, but once we arrive safely at our destination, I'm sure I'll brag about what a great trip we had."

If only she could have had Levi along, Unity knew that she would have felt completely happy, but after her dream the other night, her son hadn't left her thoughts. How empty her arms felt!

A commotion ahead made Unity notice that Matt's mule had floundered on the bank of a stream, and as she watched, the animal lurched sideways, pitching Matt into the water. Fearful at first for his safety, she stared in amazement when Matt bounded out of the stream, ran to the animal, and started kicking the mule and pounding it with his hands.

"After I finished the overland crossing four years ago, I swore I'd never deal with another mule. What a fool I was to trust one! I'm walking the rest of the way."

So here was another side of Matt Miller! She'd taken him for a quiet, even-tempered man, but she realized now it wasn't wise to make him angry. To think he'd borne a grudge against mules for years!

Although Unity escaped a fall from her mule's back, most of the other passengers ended up on the ground at least once before they completed their journey. When they reached the last hill above Panama Bay, the travelers joined in a shout of exultation. They'd made it! In six days they'd crossed the jungle, without serious mishap. Unity didn't think she'd ever seen a more unkempt group of people, but at least none of them had succumbed to jungle fevers, and dirt could soon be washed away.

"Ah, a hotel!" Calvin said with satisfaction as they entered the little port.

"Yes," Matt answered with a smile. "There's also a ship flying the Spencer flag, so perhaps we can sail northward in a few days. As soon as I've bathed and changed into clean clothes, I'll check out our passage." He turned to Unity. "You were right."

"Oh?" she said.

"You were sure that you and Loretta would make it as well as the rest of us, and you have. I'm glad now you didn't go around the Horn."

And as he looked at the mud-splattered woman beside him, Matt knew that in spite of the rigors of the journey, he wouldn't have missed traveling the Panama trail with her. Unity was the most desirable woman he'd ever known. After all his years of bachelorhood, had Matt Miller at last found a woman he wanted?

But who was Levi? Unity said her husband's name had been *Samuel;* then whom had she called for in her sleep? Could she have placed her affections elsewhere already? Even as he accepted the fact that he wanted Unity Spencer, Matt wondered if he could ever claim her.

4

*U*nity and Matt stood near the ship's prow as the *Spencer* slowly approached the coast. Five days earlier the ship had docked at Monterey, where the Swishers had disembarked, and now, thirty days after they'd left Panama City, the end of their journey lay before them. Low mountains hugged the rocky coastline to their left, but the land rose less ruggedly on the right.

As soon as the ship nosed through the narrow inlet, into the quiet waters of San Francisco Bay, the captain issued a guarded order to the first mate, and while the captain held a gun on the astonished crew, the mate clapped all the sailors in irons. The seamen's astonishment couldn't have been any greater than Matt's. "Why did you do that?" he demanded.

Although busy maneuvering the boat into harbor with only one assistant, the captain said, "Look around you. See all those ships along the waterfront? They're here because their crews have gone to the gold fields. Part of my crew deserted the last time. *No one* will leave, this trip!"

At least fifty boats lay at anchor below the old Spanish-Mexican fort that had guarded the harbor for years. Although most of them flew the United States flag, Matt spotted some lateen-rigged ships from the Mediterranean, a few with northern European flags, and at least two Chinese junks. The captain of the *Spencer* had to search for a suitable anchorage, but at last he nosed his ship in between another Spencer vessel and one bearing the flag of Spain. The first mate lowered a rowboat to ferry the passengers to the wharf.

Matt glanced around him, hardly believing that this was the sleepy village he'd left less than six months ago. Buildings had sprung up over the slopes and around the bay, and tents dotted the hills. The town swarmed with humanity, reminding Matt of a frenzied colony of ants.

When Matt left the small boat and climbed to the dock, he sensed a peculiar churning in the usually quiet water around them, and just as he reached a hand to help Unity from the boat, the earth shook and a surge of water whirled into the bay, splashing against the piers of the harbor. The anchored ships shivered as if a giant hand had swept across them. Matt stumbled on the wharf, and as he fell to his knees, he heard Unity's scream. The rowboat upended, tumbling her and the mate into the water.

Unity sank out of sight, but immediately the earth's trembling ceased, and water suctioned out of the harbor, exposing the ships' hulls. Unity was thrown, stunned, against the side of the wharf, when the water receded, but Matt gained his feet and jumped into the wet sand beside her. With the mate's help, he lifted her to the dock before the waters again splashed around the wooden piling below them.

Unity struggled to sit up, muttering, "What . . . what happened?"

"An earthquake, ma'am," the mate answered. "That caused a tidal surge. You had a narrow escape."

Unity felt around her on the dock and frantically said, "My bag? Where is it?"

The reticule had hung on her arm when she'd left the ship; it was gone now. Matt looked down at the water where she'd landed after her fall.

"I'm afraid that surge of water cleaned out the harbor. Were its contents important?"

"Yes, you might say that," she moaned. Besides a quantity of greenbacks, the reticule contained the papers proving her legal divorce from Samuel, which she'd received two days before she left Boston, as well as the daguerreotype of Levi. She didn't suppose she'd ever need the divorce papers, but how could she manage without looking at Levi's likeness every day?

John Spencer stood in the midst of a room littered with papers and upended furniture when they entered Spencer Shipping's office.

"Matt!" he cried. "Guess San Francisco gave you a rousing welcome home." Then glancing at Matt's drenched companion, he said uncertainly, "Unity?"

At her nod, he enveloped his niece in a tight embrace. He pulled back immediately. "You're wet."

"She was still in the rowboat when the earthquake hit. She's lucky she wasn't washed out to sea with the tidal surge."

"And I thought *I* had trouble," he said, sweeping his arm to indicate the littered floor. "The force of the quake tumbled me out of my chair and upended everything else.

"We'll have to see about some dry clothing for you."

"I'll go to the ship and fetch her trunks, if you can loan me a wheelbarrow. I didn't see a port worker anywhere, or I'd have hired one to bring our things."

Spencer shook his head despairingly. "Everybody's gone to the diggings. Thousands of people have traveled through this village, while you were gone. If you'd had your steamboat ready, you could have hauled plenty of people up the Sacramento."

After Matt left, John led Unity to his small bedroom, adjacent to the office. "There's water in that bucket, if you want to wash off the grime and be ready to change into dry garments when Matt returns. I'm puzzled, Unity, I thought your husband was coming with you. Didn't you marry?"

"Yes, we were married a year ago in January, but he drowned at sea a few months later. Isaac had a stroke in December, so I was the only person available to come."

"It hardly seems right for you to assume all this responsibility. I could have stayed a little longer."

"I wanted to leave anyway, Uncle John. Besides, Dad trained me in every aspect of the shipping business, and I believe I can handle the job."

As Unity removed her soiled clothing, she talked through the thin door to Spencer, giving him the details of their sea experiences as well as the trip across Panama. "It was a rough journey, and we're thankful to God that we arrived safely."

"Since you're here, I'll admit I am anxious to move to the rancho. While it's not close to the gold fields, I still fear people might swarm over it, as they have Sutter's holdings."

Matt entered the office, with Unity's trunk over his shoulder, in time to hear the last statement.

"Sutter having trouble, is he?"

"He's ruined. He doesn't have anyone to till his fields or care for the stock. There must be close to ten thousand people up there now. A town, Coloma, has sprouted on the American River, and it already contains hundreds of houses. Sutter hasn't been successful in keeping prospectors out, but he's making money selling supplies to them. He's rented all of his buildings to merchants and storekeepers. Prices have gone out of sight. I hope you brought all the supplies I ordered."

"We didn't bring them with us, but we dispatched three ships before we left. One of the ships is a clipper, and the captain said he'd reach California in three months, if his luck held. The other two will travel more slowly. They're still finding lots of gold then?"

"Yes, if the accounts are true. All of the streams are full, and many people are digging into the hills and finding riches. Money has lost all value to those people, and they'll pay any price a merchant asks. At Sutter's Fort, flour is selling at eight hundred dollars a barrel, sugar is four hundred, and it's more than a dollar for a bottle of molasses or vinegar. Here in San Francisco, people pay three dollars for a single egg, and onions can't be purchased for less than two dollars each. I tell you, people have gone crazy."

From the back room Unity had listened to their conversation, while she changed into dry clothes, and when she entered the office, she said, "It isn't good, is it, for people who've been poor all of their lives to suddenly be thrust into riches?"

"No, it's easy come, easy go. If these people would do like Matt, find the gold and invest it in some business, they'd be much better off. But most of them will keep looking for the big strike and end up penniless."

"Well, I'd better bid you good-bye and start working, if

I'm going to have that business. Do you know if Sid Green has come back from Oregon with my schooner?"

"Yes, he stopped by last week."

"I brought a small engine with me, and I'll install it on the schooner until the clipper arrives with the supplies for my steamboat." Matt held out his hand to Unity. "I guess it will be good-bye for now. I need to be on my way, and John will take care of you."

"Thank you, Matt. Your presence made the long trip much more pleasant than it would have been otherwise. Don't stay away long."

"He's a good man," John said as they watched Matt walk toward the bay.

"Yes, he has been quite attentive," Unity said, and she felt her face flush when John favored her with an appraising glance.

To cover her confusion, Unity looked around the room. "Shouldn't we do some housecleaning?"

Righting the overturned desk, John said, "This will be a good time to teach you the business, and you can organize records the way you want them. I'll not go until you think you can handle things. With so many bad characters moving in, I'm not too eager to leave you alone in this town."

"I'll manage. You've given plenty of years to Spencer Shipping; it's time you lived the way you want to. When am I going to meet your family?"

He smiled. "Soon, I hope. We'll have you to the rancho for a visit."

The San Francisco branch of the company had been operating for ten years, serving as a way station for ships from the East Coast on their way to and from the Sandwich Islands. When the ships left Boston, they were filled with molasses, tinware, and iron products for the natives on the islands. There the ships picked up products from the Orient and sailed back to San Francisco.

The California ranchos provided cattle hides and tallow for trade. The hides were turned into shoes in eastern factories, while the tallow was used in making candles, soap, and other products. Vaqueros drove their herds to the coast, where they slaughtered the animals, dried the skins, processed the fat, and waited for a ship to appear with trade stuffs. When he'd come to California ten years before, John had met his future wife as a result of buying hides from her father.

By the end of two weeks, Unity thought she'd learned as much as she could about her duties as manager of Spencer Shipping, and she insisted that John return to the ranch.

"Where are you going to live, Unity?"

"I'll live at the Fremont Hotel for the time being," she told him, "but I'll arrange something else before long. I won't continue paying twenty-five dollars a night for a room!"

"And the prices will soar above that before this gold stampede tapers off."

Although Unity didn't want John to know, her money supply was running low, because of the loss of her reticule. Once the three ships arrived with trading goods, she'd have plenty of money, but for now she had to economize. Still the room adjacent to the office where John lived was too small for Unity's needs. If San Francisco was going to be her permanent residence, she had to have a home. Looking toward the hills where a tent city had bloomed, she hoped she wouldn't be reduced to living in a tent.

Matt had made only two brief appearances at the office, for he was rushing to install the engine in his schooner, eager to start a packet business from San Francisco to the gold fields. The evening after John's departure for the rancho, Unity strolled down along the harbor before retiring to the hotel for the night.

She speculatively surveyed the two Spencer boats lying at anchor, without a crew to take them home. Matt's schooner was tied up not far from one of the Spencer ships. Stained with grease from his work on the engine, Matt appeared on deck when she called.

"Come on over," he said and laid a plank for her. She stepped hesitantly on the narrow board, panicking momentarily when she thought of her experience with the earthquake, but she made it safely across.

"You're in time for supper," Matt said. "Come in the galley; I was just washing up."

Matt introduced her to Sid Green, who was spooning beans into bowls. Sid filled a third one for her and pulled a pan of corn bread out of the oven.

"When will the boat be ready to start?" she asked as Matt settled on the bench beside her.

"Tomorrow," he answered calmly, but excitement shone from his eyes. "We took the schooner out for a trial run today, up the river about five miles, and everything works the way it's supposed to. We won't have much freight, this trip, but eight prospectors have booked passage. I'm eager to see what's happened along the rivers since I left. John gone?"

"Yes, he left this morning, so I'm on my own. I've been wondering what to do about lodgings. Since it doesn't look as if those two ships of ours will be going anyplace soon, is there any reason I couldn't convert one of them into a dwelling? With a little carpentry work, I could turn that smaller ship into comfortable living space."

"It may be a good idea. I worry about your being here

alone, but the boat is as safe as any other place. Maybe safer, since you can pull in the gangplank to discourage easy access."

"I intend to find some help. I need someone to work at the office part of the time, and I could use a housekeeper. I can't run the business and operate a home, too."

Matt walked back to the hotel with her, and when they arrived there after a roundabout jaunt, she said, "How long will you be gone?"

"A couple of weeks, maybe. If the engine works correctly, we might make even better time, but I want to look around a bit on this trip."

"I'll miss you, Matt. Come to see me when you return."

He squeezed her hand, lifted it to his face, and a flush of pleasure spread through her body. "I don't think you'll ever be rid of me now. I'm going to miss you, too." He placed a slight kiss on her fingers before he turned away.

Finding a carpenter wasn't an easy task, Unity learned the next day, when she made inquiries for someone to remodel the ship into living quarters. The town was practically devoid of able-bodied men, and those who remained were merchants.

Determined to remodel the ship, Unity found lumber and nails in the Spencer warehouse and hired a Mexican laborer to haul them to the ship. She had decided to tackle the project herself when an Oriental couple appeared in the office.

The man stepped forward and bowed. "Missy looking for carpenter?" he said in broken English.

"Yes, I am."

He clapped his hands, and the woman at the door eased outside, to reenter, carrying a table. She bowed as she placed it on the floor beside Unity. The table was of black ebony, highly lacquered, with a bright-yellow lotus-blossom inlay.

"Did you make this?"

The man bobbed his head, and the thin pigtail hanging down his back swung like a pendulum.

"This is a beautiful table, and I'll be happy to have you do my carpentry work. What's your name?"

"Soong Lin, from Peking," he answered. Following the Chinese custom, he had put his last name first. "My woman is Soong Jiang. Jiang help me with the work."

"Very well, Mr. Soong. Let's go to the harbor, and I'll explain what I want done."

Unity noticed that Soong Jiang shuffled her feet, and she slowed to a stroll. "How long have you been in California?"

Holding up one finger, Jiang answered in English more broken than her husband's, "One month. Leave China for Sandwich Islands two years ago. Chinese there hear about gold, so come fast, fast to get some."

Lin pointed to the sampan lying at anchor.

"How many of you?" asked Unity.

"Twenty-six. All gone to gold fields except us."

With a smile, Unity asked, "Aren't you interested in finding gold?"

"Jiang no have good feet." He pointed at his wife's misshapen feet, which Unity surmised had been caused by the custom of binding women's feet in China. "Besides, got daughter, not want to take to mountains."

"Daughter work at hotel," his wife added.

Unity remembered that she had seen a young Chinese woman working in the hotel's kitchen.

After giving instructions of what she wanted done on the boat, Unity gave free rein to the Chinese couple, and in three weeks she was amazed at the floating palace they'd created for her. The entire deck had been enclosed in a four-room edifice. Admittedly, from the outside, the houseboat had a distinctively Oriental appearance, with an oval roof displaying rounded ends that resembled a pagoda.

A dining room adjoined the galley. The living area comprised the mid-section of the ship, and windows resembling huge portholes gave Unity a view of the harbor as well as of the wharf. Her bedroom opened off the living room. Below deck, Lin had provided quarters for his family, for Unity didn't like the idea of living alone around the harbor.

Lin had also made furniture, which Jiang covered with silk tapestries that Unity found in the warehouse of Spencer Shipping. She moved into the houseboat, eagerly awaiting Matt's opinion when he returned from the gold fields. He arrived late in the day, and she waved to him from the walkway Lin had left around the cabin.

Unity laughed at the amazement mirrored on the faces of Matt and Sid, and when Matt came to check out the transformation, he said, "I must have been away longer than I thought. Did you have a fairy godmother do all of this?"

"No, it's magic wrought by two Chinese. Sit down, and I'll serve you some tea. Tea seems the appropriate drink in this type of setting."

Unity poured the tea from a set of porcelain utensils she'd also found in the warehouse, and Matt held the dainty cup awkwardly. Laughing at him, she returned to the kitchen and brought out a tin cup. "Would you prefer this?"

Sitting across from him, with a low, hand-carved table between them, she commented, "You've been gone over three weeks. Did you have trouble?"

"No. I couldn't believe the change in that country, and I took time to look around. A year ago, discounting the Indians, there weren't more than a thousand people living in this whole area. I'll judge there are ten times that many in the gold fields now."

"Where did they come from? How could the news travel so rapidly?"

"A lot of people have come in from Oregon and southern California, and many American soldiers stayed on after the war with Mexico ended. Large numbers of foreigners have come in on these ships, heard about the gold, and headed that way."

"How's Captain Sutter reacting?"

"His normal farming chores have ceased, but the fort has become a stopping place for gold seekers, and he's selling supplies as fast as he unpacks them. He's rented all of his buildings to merchants at high prices."

"Are they *finding* gold or only *looking*?"

"Rich deposits have been found all along the American River, the Feather River, and the Yuba. Those streams are tributaries of the Sacramento. We left my boat at the fort and went to the site where Marshall found gold. Houses are going up by the hundreds, and Sutter's sawmill is busy turning out lumber for new buildings and stores for the new town, Coloma."

"I'm surprised Sid came back with you, when gold is so plentiful."

"Sid admits he's too lazy to dig for gold, and that's good news for me. We're going back upriver in a few days, and we'll take anything you want to sell."

"I'll look through the warehouse tomorrow."

"Any of the ships come in yet?"

"No, and I rather thought the clipper might be here by now."

Placing his cup on the table, Matt said, "While we're tied up for a few days, this would be a good chance for us to visit John's rancho. When the clipper comes in, you're going to be busy. Could you go tomorrow?"

"Yes, if you don't mind my putting off inspecting the warehouse. And it might be a convenient time to go, for one of Uncle John's vaqueros and his wife are in town, buying supplies. They're returning tomorrow, and we could ride along with them."

"That should work out well then," Matt said. "I'll make arrangements to rent a couple of horses and a pack mule."

Taking her hand, Matt pulled her close. Her eyes were on a level with his, and his gaze, meeting hers, held a wistful expression.

"The trip upriver was lonely without you, Unity. I'd gotten used to your company during the past few months. How long does a man have to know a woman before he falls in love with her?"

"I don't know, but when you decide, you might let me know," she said with a laugh, but her heartbeat accelerated.

A flush darkened his face as Matt placed a light kiss on her laughing lips and left the room hurriedly.

An hour before they reached their destination, the travelers saw the Alvarado rancho, which was situated on a high knoll. Before they rode through the adobe walls, Matt motioned westward, and in spite of her sore muscles and numb limbs and a desire to leave the saddle, Unity halted her horse.

"What a view! No wonder Uncle John wants to live here."

The broad expanse of the Pacific spread before them, and white-capped breakers surged against the beach. Sea otters played in the surf washing upon the white sand. The scene reminded Unity of the dreams she'd had before she came to California. Had her life finally become peaceful?

When they rode into the courtyard of the sprawling, adobe structure, dozens of laughing people, chattering in Spanish, immediately surrounded them.

"Hello," someone shouted, and Unity saw John striding toward them. He lifted her out of the saddle and held on to her when she started to collapse.

"Don't have your land legs yet?" He laughed and led her toward the veranda, where a plump Mexican woman with sparkling black eyes curtsied before them.

"This is Maria, and here are my son and daughter," he said as two children peered shyly from the house. "Carmen, Raoul, come meet your cousin Unity."

Raoul, the older of the two, bore the Spencer features, with only a slight darkening of his skin to show his mother's heritage. His reddish hair and brown eyes saddened Unity, for she knew she'd never see Levi when he was this age. Carmen, who looked about four years old, was purely Spanish in appearance.

"They're beautiful children, Uncle. No wonder you're proud of them."

Unity looked over the courtyard, where dozens of riderless horses stood with dragging reins and countless natives lolled in the shade of the palm trees, while others worked slowly to unsaddle the horses she and Matt had ridden.

"Who are all these people, Uncle?"

Laughing boisterously, he said, "Don't ask me. They're somebody's cousins or brothers or sisters. I've never tried to keep track of them."

Inside the house, Unity was introduced to Stephano

Alvarado, John's father-in-law, a stately old man with white hair and an erect bearing. He bowed low and said in heavily accented English, "Welcome to our humble home."

Unity sighed when she was shown to a cool room, a pleasant change after the hot sun they'd ridden through all day. Shutters were drawn across the one window, but light showing through the slats revealed whitewashed walls and a tempting bed hung with colorful curtains. A cheerful maid entered the room with an earthenware pitcher of steaming water. Next a boy carried in the saddlebags containing her clothing.

Unity relaxed on the soft bed a few minutes, but she roused herself as her eyes grew heavy. After bathing and changing into clean garments, she went to the veranda where John and Matt talked.

"Let's walk around before the meal is served. Walking is the best thing for stiff joints," John invited.

During their stroll, Unity observed that the rancho combined Spanish romance and charm with what she thought of as John's New England thrift. Acres of grapes grew along one sunny slope, while orange, lemon, and fig trees filled an orchard. A few cultivated fields yielded grain and vegetables, and in the corral milk cattle grazed contentedly.

John pointed out a cobbler's shop where steer hides were turned into shoes for the rancho's population.

With a worried look, John turned to Matt. "Do you think the gold craze will reach this far? I've heard what's happening to Sutter, and I'd hate to see gold hunters move in here."

"It might be a good idea to keep your vaqueros on patrol most of the time, and John, have you thought of asking the United States government for a deed to this property?

Alvarado's Spanish grant might not hold up under Yankee ownership."

John nodded sagely. "I had the same idea. I went to see Walter Colton, the new American governor in Monterey, and he recognized my problem. He gave me a set of papers to uphold our claim, and he's sending copies to authorities in Washington. I think we're all right, as long as some prospector doesn't find a pocket of gold near us."

Dinner was served at twilight, and the soft glow of candles flickered over the faces of the Alvarado family and their guests. In the courtyard, a guitarist strummed softly, adding to the tranquility of the scene. After they dined, the Americans joined the natives on the patio to watch as the young men and women, dressed in garments of vivid reds, yellows, and black, performed a rollicking dance. Guitars and castanets provided the rhythm, and a dozen youth exhibited skillful footwork, finger snapping, and forceful, flowing arm movements.

The dancers communicated their vivacity to Unity, and she clapped in time to the music. Matt looked at her quizzically. "Do you want to try it?"

"Not me. I'd collapse on the first stamp, but it's beautiful." Turning to John, she said, "Do they do this every evening?"

"We have lots of music around here, but this is a special performance, because we have guests."

Unity experienced a tinge of sadness as she surveyed her tranquil surroundings. In a few years such scenes would become rare in California, for American culture would quickly submerge this slow, rich Spanish heritage. Yet she was thankful that she'd had the opportunity to witness the old way of life.

5

*T*he two days at the rancho had rested Unity somewhat, but she dreaded their return journey to San Francisco, for her legs still felt the effects of that long horseback ride.

"We'll go at an easy pace, so you'll be all right," Matt assured her as they set out in an early morning fog rolling in from the Pacific.

"How did you become such an expert horseman, when you've spent most of your life on boats?"

"I don't consider myself an expert horseman. You'll know what that means when you see some vaqueros racing, but I learned to ride when I crossed the continent to Oregon, several years ago."

"Why did you decide to come West?"

"My sister, Becky, had a problem, and I thought I needed to remove her from danger. As it turned out, the problem wasn't serious, but I'm not sorry I left the East. I like it out here."

"Where's Becky now?"

"She's happily married, living on a ranch not far from Oregon City. They have a son now."

A reverent tone graced Matt's voice when he spoke Becky's name, and Unity said, teasingly, "Pretty fond of her, aren't you?"

He flushed slightly and admitted, "I'd do anything for her, but she doesn't need me now. She has a good husband to take care of her. Otherwise, I wouldn't have considered moving to California."

"She may not need you, but do *you* need her?"

"I guess so. She's much younger than I am, and she was my responsibility for years after our mother's death. I haven't gotten over wanting to take care of her, but I like her husband, and he appreciates her, knows he has a woman in a million."

"Apparently you don't think other women are in her class."

Pulling his horse close to hers, Matt took Unity's hand. "I've only seen one other to rival Becky, and I think you know who that is. I can't comprehend yet what's happened to me, Unity. Never before have I met a woman to whom I've given the least attention, but you're with me all the time, whether or not I'm around you. Am I moving too fast for you?"

She withdrew her hand and moved her horse forward. "What traits do you expect a woman to have?"

"What any man wants, I suppose. Chastity, honesty, and loyalty. But I'm not worried about any of those things with you." He paused, then said, "I know it isn't any of my business, but are you still in love with your husband?"

She threw him a startled gaze. "I *never* loved Samuel Whitley. That marriage was arranged by my father. It may shock you, but since you value truthfulness in a woman, I'll tell you, I was glad to get rid of him."

"Are you in love with any other man?"

"Why, no! What would give you that idea?"

Matt didn't answer, but he still wondered who Levi was.

Still conscious of Matt's questioning appraisal, when the trail narrowed, she urged her mount forward to forestall any more conversation. If Matt prized truthfulness and honesty, he wouldn't have any use for her. In her heart, Unity knew that now was the time to tell him about her life with Samuel and the birth of Levi, but she had a feeling that Matt wouldn't approve of a mother who gave away her child. She liked the admiration she received from him, and she didn't want to spoil their relationship. Would he ever have to know about Levi? After all, she had promised Margaret she'd keep it a secret.

Two days after Matt started his second trip upriver to the gold fields, the Spencer clipper ship sailed into port. Begging merchants immediately converged on the ship, because supplies in San Francisco had diminished sharply in the past few weeks as more and more immigrants sailed through the Golden Gate.

Unity enlisted help from the sailors to store all the supplies from the ship in the Spencer warehouse. After the goods were unloaded, Unity secretly advised the captain, "If you don't want to lose your crew, pull out of here as soon as you can provision. Otherwise, most of these men will head for the gold fields." Motioning to the numerous abandoned ships in the harbor, she added, "That's why none of those ships is leaving; not one has a crew."

In two days the clipper sailed, carrying letters from Unity to Isaac Smith, with orders for more supplies. She also wrote to Deborah Jenkins, begging for news of Levi, but her heart sank when she considered that, even barring trouble, it would be six months or more before a clipper could bring any news of her child. She wished she'd never given the boy to Margaret, especially now, when she suspected that she was in love with the truth-loving Matt.

The local merchants became frantic when they saw the large load of lumber the clipper had brought, but much of it belonged to Matt for his steamboat. Unity wasn't at liberty to sell any of it, but she did store it in her warehouse, along with the engine, fearing theft if she left it at the dock.

Organizing the shipment of goods took several days. Unity hired Jiang and Lin to help her, but she realized the enormity of the job she'd undertaken. The teas, coffee, and sugar, along with raisins and molasses, she shelved for Matt's trade. As she unpacked she appreciated John's foresight, for he had ordered plenty of items needed by gold seekers, and the other two ships would carry similar provisions. Unity sold the clothing, boots, and shoes to the merchants at a reasonable profit, and she felt relief at having funds again.

With her financial problems solved, Unity thought she would be free from concern, until she learned from Lin that several of the Chinese had been driven from the gold fields.

"Scared away," he said. "Miners don't like Chinese. Treated bad. Now nothing to do and no money to go back."

"How were they treated?"

"Pigtails cut off. Beat them. Said gold for Americans."

"You bring your friends to me. There are more ways to accumulate gold than to dig for it. I don't need anyone here except you and Jiang, but we'll see they find something to do."

"Most can't speak American."

"We'll do something about that, too."

That evening as she walked around the streets of San Francisco and along the wharf, Unity saw long lines of men waiting in front of a restaurant for a meal; other men washed their clothes in a stream that flowed into the bay. Her head full of ideas, Unity faced the fifteen Chinese who came to the warehouse the next morning.

Lin haltingly translated her words to his friends. "How many of you would like to operate a restaurant?" Two held up their hands. "Is there anyone who could launder clothing?" When these words were translated, three Chinese nodded emphatically and chattered to Lin. Their high-pitched voices grated on Unity's nerves, but she'd decided on this course of action, and she intended to see it through. She would train these people to be productive citizens in their adopted home.

To her amazement, they responded quickly to her teaching, and by the time Matt returned, some of them were able to speak a few words in the English language and were actually operating businesses of their own. She'd allowed the laundry gang, as she called them, to set up shop in the other abandoned Spencer ship, and for the restaurant, she'd erected a huge tent close by the Fremont Hotel. With their friends operating the restaurant, Lin and Jiang had removed their daughter from the hotel kitchen, so she could work in the new restaurant, a move that had earned Unity, as well as the Chinese, a torrent of censure from the hotel's manager. Help of any kind was almost nonexistent, and he didn't appreciate losing Wang. The remainder of the Orientals started work on the hotel that Unity planned to build.

Two Bibles were the only books Unity had, and after she taught the Chinese their basic letters and words, she copied down Bible verses for them to read. The difference between English letters and the Chinese characters made it much more difficult for them to learn to read than to speak.

When Jiang had mastered the words "For God so loved the world, that he gave his only begotten Son, that whosoever believeth in him should not perish, but have eternal life," she turned to Unity. "I do not know this God and His Son. The Chinese have many gods. We take offerings to the gods. Sometimes they receive them; sometimes they do not."

"There is only one God, Jiang." Unity held up the Bible. "When you have acquired a little more knowledge of English, you can read from this Book the story of God and His Son."

Matt lovingly ran his hand over the smooth oak lumber and peered into the crate that housed the engine. "I'll start on my boat right away. The sooner I put it into operation, the better off I'll be. The gold fields are swarming with people now, but when the cold winter rains start, they won't be satisfied to live in tents. They'll travel to San Francisco to spend their gold dust, and I mean to provide their transportation."

"How long will it take to build the boat?"

"Depends on what kind of help I find. Carpenters are scarce around here. Sid will continue the river trade with the schooner, and I'll stay here to supervise the building of the boat, but I'll need help."

"Why not use Soong Lin and his friends?" She'd already explained to Matt about her Chinese project, so he knew whom she meant.

"Well, he did a good job on your houseboat, and the

Chinese have been building ships for a long time. It's worth a try."

Matt drew her into his arms, and Unity leaned her head on his shoulder.

"Missed me?" he asked.

"Of course."

"Unity, you're the only woman I've ever wanted to marry. Do you love me enough for that?"

"You don't know much about me, Matt. We haven't talked about the past."

"Nothing you tell me is going to make any difference in my wanting you. I don't think about anything else. I remind myself of a half-grown boy, instead of a man."

"We wouldn't have much of a life, with you traveling on the river and with me tied to Spencer Shipping."

"You should have some help."

"I have Lin and Jiang."

"Yes, but I mean an American, who could give you a break once in a while. I'd like to visit John again, but I don't suppose you could leave."

"Not when I'm expecting those two ships any day. But I would welcome an assistant, if we can find one who's not chasing off to the gold fields."

The hull of Matt's boat took shape quickly under the skillful hands of Lin and his countrymen, and while the Chinese completed the carpentry work, Matt installed the engine. Unity leaned on the rail of her houseboat one evening, watching the workers, when she became aware that the Spencer ship on the Panama run had just dropped anchor in the harbor.

She hurried to the wharf, arriving just as a boat from the *Spencer* reached the shoreline. A tall, lanky boy, with a lean face and hollow eyes, stepped from the boat.

"Can you direct me to Miss Unity Spencer?" he questioned. Once she'd identified herself, he continued, "I'm Alex Smith, a nephew of Isaac. I've a letter from him concerning me." He handed the missive to Unity. Breaking the seal, she read Isaac's sprawling scribbles.

Unity:

Since you left, I've been concerned about your being in charge of the business out there without any help at all. A doctor suggested that a sea voyage might improve my nephew's health, and I'm sending him on the next boat. Try to put him to work if you can. With his ailment, he won't be apt to take off gold hunting, and I think you'll be pleased with his work.

Unfortunately, my health has not improved, and I sometimes despair that I'll ever be well again. Levi and Margaret both remain in good health.

Isaac

Unity appraised the boy. She needed a man who could handle crates and barrels, and Alex didn't look physically fit.

"Did the sea voyage improve your health, Alex?"

"No, ma'am, it didn't. I was seasick the whole trip, and crossing the isthmus almost did me in. I picked up malaria."

"What's your physical trouble?"

"Weak lungs. If you're wondering what I can do, I've been trained as a bookkeeper."

Unity made an instantaneous decision. "I can use a good bookkeeper. Come over to my houseboat, and I'll feed you. Uncle John lived in a small room in our warehouse, and I think it will be adequate for your needs." She extended her hand. "Welcome to California, Alex."

As she prepared him a light meal, Alex reached in his satchel. "I have other letters for you."

The letters were from Margaret and Deborah, but although her heart raced when she received them, she forced herself to place food in front of him before she opened the letters.

"Now, if you'll excuse me, it's been a long time since I've heard from my family."

She opened Deborah's letter first.

Miss Unity,

All is well here. Levi is growing strong and healthy. The nurse and I have almost the full care of the child now, since Isaac requires more and more of Margaret's attention. As you know, she soon tires of anything new, and she has lost interest in Levi, but you may be assured that I'm taking good care of the child.

Deborah

Tears stung Unity's eyes, but she breathed a prayer of thanks for Deborah. At least Levi was loved. Was Margaret capable of loving anyone?

Margaret's letter was a brief, cold missive stating that Levi was well, that Isaac's health seemed to deteriorate steadily rather than to improve, and that he sent his best regards to Unity. The closing, "Your loving sister, Margaret," seemed ironic, but knowing Margaret, Unity accepted the letter, grateful that it was no worse.

The messages brought Unity no peace of mind, because when she'd agreed for Margaret to take her son, she'd counted on the steady hand of Isaac Smith to control both Margaret and Levi. If Isaac was an invalid, the household would not be a good place for the child.

Right from the first, Alex Smith became a help to Unity. Soon after his arrival, the two ships she'd awaited came in loaded with supplies, and Unity hardly knew what she would have done without his help. The warehouse was packed with merchandise, and with the prices asked in the stores now, Unity needed someone on guard at all times.

Not only was Alex good with figures, but his presence in the office at night served as extra security for the supplies. Although she thought of him as a boy, Alex wasn't that much younger than she, and he'd assumed a man's role immediately. Upon his arrival, he'd pulled a wicked-looking gun from his trunk and propped it on the table by his bed. "I'll patrol a time or two at night, ma'am, and I'm a light sleeper. No need to worry."

Matt helped with the unloading of the ships whenever he could spare time from his construction, but the steamboat was rapidly nearing completion. With the limited help they had, it took over a week to unload Unity's two ships, and by that time many of the sailors had deserted to the gold fields. Considering all the other ships lying idle in the harbor, though loss of a ship meant loss of income, Unity considered it fortunate that they had enough crew to take one of the boats back to Boston. She gave the captain orders for more supplies, for the way people were converging upon San Francisco, she was sure the Spencer warehouse would be empty before the ship returned.

Matt set the first day of November for the maiden voyage of his steamboat. With pride in his heart and with trembling hands, Matt traced the letters *Allegheny* across the side of the pilothouse. Later, viewing his handiwork from the bank, he thought he'd never seen a more beautiful sight.

When he gave Unity her first tour of the boat, he felt like a boy showing off his new toy.

"Why the name *Allegheny?*" she asked.

"That was the name of the last boat I owned on the Ohio." Leading her into the pilothouse, he rubbed his hands lovingly over the whistle installed there. "I took this whistle off the *Allegheny* when I started west and transported it across the continent. When we reached the Rockies and the mules were so weak they could hardly pull the wagon, Becky dragged the whistle on a little sled."

Matt's throat tightened when he remembered Becky's determination that he'd not leave his beloved whistle lying beside the trail. His joy would be complete if only Becky stood beside him when he guided this new boat away from the port, but Unity's presence made up for the loss of his sister.

"I thought I could start a transportation service on the Columbia, but things didn't work out that way. Yet I kept the whistle, believing that someday I'd have my steamboat again."

In the galley, the Chinese cook, Chang, bowed low when they entered, and Unity sat opposite Matt at the table. Before they ate the meal that Chang placed before them, Matt said, "I want to pray, Unity. God has brought the dreams to pass—not in the way I'd thought and not as soon as I'd hoped, but He's given me what I want in His way."

"I'm glad, Matt. You deserve some happiness, and I don't think you've had much."

He reached his hand to her. "There's only one thing I need to complete my happiness, and you know what it is."

Unity's eyes wouldn't meet his, and Matt puzzled as he had for the past two months. He loved Unity, and at times he thought she loved him, but when he pressed her for a decision, she hesitated or evaded the question.

"I'm still thinking about it, Matt. I'll give you an answer before too long."

Matt's disappointment was keen, for he had hoped that his great day of achievement would be crowned with Unity agreeing to become his wife. Something held her back. At least she hadn't said no, though, so he thanked God for all the other blessings that had come his way.

While they ate, Matt commented, "When I dreamed of operating a steamboat again, in my wildest imagination, I didn't think that my crew would be Chinese."

"It will work out all right, won't it?"

"I don't see why not. Most of those men came across the Pacific in decrepit ships that I wouldn't take across San Francisco Bay. My biggest fear was how Sid would handle it, but he does well with the new crew. I've given him one-fourth interest in the business, for I depend on him, and I'd hate to have him leave me for the diggings."

A smiling Chang hovered over them until they were finished, and then he whisked away the dishes and placed a steaming bowl of tea before them.

"How are your Chinese projects going?"

"Well enough, but the more of them I help, the more Chinese show up. I think a new boatload must come in every day."

"I walked uptown last night and noticed that your hotel is about completed."

"Yes, I figure it will be ready for occupancy by the time the *Allegheny* returns from Sutter's Fort."

"And I have a feeling I'll bring a load of cold, wet, dirty miners ready for a few months of hotel living."

"Let's hope they have their pockets full of gold. It's cost a lot of money to build that hotel, but at least I have a loyal staff. We'll give good service. So, if you have any passengers, direct them to the Spencer Hotel."

"Will you try to manage that as well as the shipping business? I can see why you won't marry me; you're too busy to take on a husband as well as two businesses and about fifty Chinese."

Unity laughed but refused to rise to his bait. "With Alex to help me, I think I can manage. I'm delighted with the interest he's shown in teaching the Chinese to read, and he's been a help also when I've tried to instruct them about Christianity. With a culture that has a blend of religions as well as a multiplicity of gods, it's difficult for the Chinese to comprehend that there is only *one* God."

Unity thanked Chang for the good meal and moved with Matt toward his stateroom. Sid also had a small cabin, but the crew would bunk below deck. The room was small and housed only a bed, dresser, and a desk that had been built by Lin, but Matt indicated it with pride. Unity sat in the only chair, while Matt leaned on the bed.

"Unity," he said hesitantly, "have you noticed any hostility from the townspeople lately?"

"Some of them have been irate because I wouldn't sell Spencer's supplies for low prices. They complain that I'm charging them more than they can get from their customers, but I know it's going to be harder and harder to have supplies shipped in. I intend to hold what we have until they're willing to pay for them. Several of Lin's relatives help Alex guard the warehouse every night."

"But have you heard any nasty remarks concerning your friendliness toward the Chinese?"

"Not that I'd noticed."

"Sid spends some time in the saloons when we're in port, and he's heard frightening comments. Seems there's a lot of resentment because you're giving the Chinese so much attention; they have good incomes, while others are barely able to buy necessities. Sid's even been taunted because we've hired a Chinese crew."

Anger crossed Unity's face. "But nobody else will work. They're here for a few days, and then they head for the gold fields. You can't depend on them."

Matt held up his hand and smiled at her. "Don't growl at me. I know that, but I wanted you to be aware of what's going on. There's a hard element moving into California now. Yesterday a boat arrived from Australia, and I'd be willing to bet most of the passengers were straight out of prison. Up until now, everything has been peaceful in the gold fields, but that time may be over."

"The merchants have been complaining about the Hounds, a group of ex-soldiers from New York who are plundering some of the stores, and Alex heard that Mexican bandits have been robbing travelers; how can we handle all this?"

"I wish we had law protection. It's still pretty much everyone for himself. I didn't mention this to worry you, but please, be careful."

By six o'clock the next morning, the *Allegheny* was ready to leave. When the five passengers he'd contracted to take on the maiden voyage came aboard, Matt motioned for a Chinese deckhand to lift the gangplank. From the boiler room, he heard the chug of the engine. As he gripped the wheel with his right hand and lifted his left hand to the whistle's chain, Matt's eyes misted, sweat moistened his face and hands, and his breath erupted laboriously from his chest.

The melodious whistle caught the attention of dock workers, and Matt had an audience as he backed carefully from the wharf. Only one onlooker concerned Matt, and he shifted his gaze momentarily to Unity's houseboat, where she leaned over the rail, waving to him. She lifted her hand and threw him a kiss. Matt returned the gesture, then quickly transferred his attention to the boat.

Out in the open water of the bay, Matt maneuvered the boat upstream and signaled for full steam ahead. The smooth movement of the boat under his feet exhilarated Matt so that he wanted to shout, but he merely patted the wheel and smiled.

He turned when Sid Green entered the pilothouse. "How's she doing, boss?"

"Wonderful. We did a good job of building, Sid."

"I can't get over these Chinamen. You'd think they'd spent all their lives on a steamboat. I feel as if I've come home, Matt. I've never been really satisfied since I left the Mississippi River, ten years ago."

Matt didn't answer, but he knew what Sid meant. At last he'd reached the destination he'd sought since eighteen hundred forty-four.

Three days later, when they docked in front of Sutter's Fort, Matt was convinced that the *Allegheny* was a sound vessel and that his fortune was secured. Even before they landed, unkempt miners surged onboard, begging for supplies.

"Get off," Sid Green shouted, "or we won't sell you nary an item. We've got to tie up this boat."

Sullenly the miners backed off, and Matt faced a week of haggling over prices and selling the goods. The miners were desperate for food and clothing, as well as for mining equipment. Since most payment was in gold dust, Sid and Matt worked out a system of exchange, calculating one ounce of gold dust as equivalent to ten dollars in United States money. So that the miner would know in advance how much he would receive for his poke of dust, Matt listed his prices on a board:

Molasses	$1.00 a bottle
Vinegar	$1.00 a bottle
Flour	$1.00 a pound
Boots	$15.00 to $50.00, depending on choice
Wool hat	$12.00 each
Frying pan	$6.00 each
Coffeepot	$10.00 each
Candles	$1.25 each
Onions	$1.00 each

Within three days, the supplies were gone, and Matt stashed the gold dust in his stateroom.

"Do you think we'd better guard that?" Sid asked.

"I suppose one of us should be on board at all times. So far there doesn't seem to be much stealing, but gold is easy to find now. Easier to pick it up than to go to the trouble of stealing it."

"One miner told me it isn't so plentiful now, for most of the easy placer gold has been picked up from the creeks. He said there are thousands of miners in these mountains, and most of them aren't finding any gold."

"So we'd better guard what we have. I want to see Captain Sutter, and after that I'll stay on deck, if you want to look around. We'll remain here for another two days, and I think we'll have plenty of miners for Unity's hotel when we leave. Several have asked about passage, but I don't want to take more than twelve."

Matt encountered John Sutter on his way to the fort, and he was amazed at the difference in the man. In the two months since he'd seen Sutter, the trader's hair had become streaked with gray and he'd lost weight. Weary eyes peered at Matt from dark sockets. Sutter was only a shadow of the dapper man he'd been before gold was discovered.

"How are things, Captain?"

"They couldn't be worse, Mr. Miller. At first, I was making money selling to the miners, but there's a new settlement starting up the river that's taking most of my business. People have settled on my land without even asking for permission, and many of the merchants who rented my buildings are moving up to the new town. I'm ruined. I don't think I'll ever have any peace again."

When Matt returned to the *Allegheny*, he kicked the bags of gold dust he'd accumulated. He supposed as long as miners were willing to pay outlandish prices for goods, he hadn't done anything wrong, but he felt sorry for Sutter. How many more men would be ruined before this gold craze had run its course? Thinking of his own attitude, when he found the gold pockets on the mountain, he realized it was only by the grace of God that he'd come to his senses before he became obsessed with the greed for gold.

Right now, his only obsession was his need for Unity, and he wondered anew why she wouldn't marry him. She certainly wasn't mourning for her husband, for she'd said she'd felt no love for him, but something in the past seemed to haunt her.

"Missy, missy," Lin cried as he pounded on the door of her houseboat. "Big fire."

Unity opened the door on the excited man. "Where?"

"Hotel. Come."

Without waiting to put on a coat, Unity ran by Lin's side toward the hotel. Smoke billowed from the side of the building. Before they reached it, a bucket brigade had formed, and the fire was soon extinguished, but the kitchen of the new hotel was a blackened ruin. If she hadn't insisted that the kitchen be separated from the hotel by a covered walkway, the whole building would have burned.

A merchant who lived beside the hotel walked to her side. "It must have been set, Miss Spencer. Your cook saw a man running from the back of the hotel when he arrived to start work. Lots of dirty happenings in the city now."

Unity clinched her fingers and stared at the shell, knowing that this had been directed against the Chinese more than herself, for her hotel staff was comprised of about twenty Orientals.

With glinting eyes, her words brusque, she said, "They needn't think this is going to stop me. I still have some lumber; we'll rebuild and have this hotel ready by the time Matt returns."

Turning rapidly, she called to Lin, "Tell Alex to send nails and lumber up here immediately."

With downcast eyes the merchant warned, "People kinda think you're making too much of the foreigners, miss, teaching them to read and write and such. Lots of white folks in this town can't read and write; maybe you'd better back off."

Eyes snapping dangerously, Unity said, "No, I won't."

The work on the hotel's kitchen was completed in a few days, and Unity placed guards around it and all of her buildings. She protected the property, but she couldn't do much about the citizens who bullied the Chinese, and she often wondered if she was doing them more harm than good.

6

*M*att made two more trips up the Sacramento River before Christmas, and each time he brought back miners who'd had enough of the gold fields, at least until spring. Rain had been falling for over a month, flooding the streams and halting mining operations. Unity's hotel, as well as other lodging houses, filled to capacity, and men begged for rooms, willing to pay any price as long as their gold lasted.

In mid-December, however, Unity's joy over her successful business ventures dimmed when she received a letter from Margaret. Isaac Smith had died, and Unity truly mourned the man who'd been a brother to her for several years. Coupled with her sorrow over his loss was her concern for Levi, left with Margaret as his only parent.

Before Unity could send word of Isaac's death to her Uncle John, he came to San Francisco. John entered the shipping office where Alex and Unity were balancing accounts. Two vaqueros followed him, carrying baskets of plums, figs, and apples.

"Thought this might be a help with your Christmas feasting, and I also have a haunch of beef out in the cart."

"It's time you paid us a visit," Unity said. "How do you like the new San Francisco?"

"I can't believe there's such a change in a village." A stunned look accompanied his words. "The vaqueros had been telling me about this influx of humanity, but I had to see for myself. This place is a beehive."

"At least six thousand people are wintering here," Unity said. "We've had dribbles of emigrants from the East Coast, where the news is gradually spreading, many people from the west coast of South America, and some from Asia. Besides the Chinese, who've tried the gold fields and then come back to work for Matt and me, many Asians are still trying to make it rich by digging. How are things at the rancho? Any trouble there?"

"No, I think we're too far south for much concern, but several ranchos near the gold fields have been plundered. Not only have the gold seekers taken over the land, they've killed cattle, stolen horses, and torn down buildings to run up shacks for themselves. I tell you this gold rush is the ruination of California, and it makes me sick."

"Come for supper tonight at my houseboat. You haven't even seen it. I'll invite Matt, too."

As Unity waited for John and Matt to come that evening, she fretted, *What answer am I going to give Matt?* More and more, he was pressing her to become his wife. She loved him and wanted to marry him, but how could she live a lie? When she had promised Margaret that she'd keep the circumstances of Levi's birth a secret, she had not considered remarriage. How could she marry Matt without telling him she'd borne a son?

Always in the back of her mind lay the fact that Samuel's body had never been recovered. Of course, she had the divorce, so legally she was free from him, whether or not he lived, but would remarriage be right in God's eyes? How would Matt feel about it? She'd learned already that he expected unreproachable behavior from a woman, and she no longer had the papers to prove she was divorced. In her last letter to Deborah, she'd asked her to obtain copies and send them along, but that could take months.

Before his arrival at San Francisco, John had stopped overnight in Monterey, and at supper, he delivered greetings from the Swishers. "Mrs. Swisher is quite lonely, and she'd like you to pay them a visit."

"It may be best if they came to visit me, but I will write them."

John left for the rancho the next morning, but he pressed an invitation on Unity and Matt. "Why not come for Christmas? We do a bit of celebrating then."

Matt shook his head. "No, I don't want to be away during Christmas and New Year's Day. These miners may go on a rampage during their celebrating, and I must be here to protect my property. We could come in January, if Unity is willing. There won't be much activity in the gold fields until April, but I'll start my run again around the first of February."

"I can leave for a few days," Unity agreed, "but I'd like Alex to have a break, so will you invite him to come up later?"

"Alex," Unity said a few days before Christmas. "As much as I've tried, I can't teach the Chinese the true meaning of Christianity. If we had them participate in a pageant portraying the birth of Christ, do you think they might receive a better understanding of our faith?"

"It's worth a try. Several of them have an adequate command of the language, so they should be able to learn small speaking parts."

"And after the performance, we can have a feast for them. I'll teach Jiang how to make plum pudding, if we can find the ingredients." Unity made notes on a tablet as they talked. "Let's tally our ideas."

"'We could gather in the warehouse; it's almost empty again."

"Perhaps we can use Mexican blankets for costumes."

"When the Chinese come for their lessons, this afternoon, I'll tell them what we want to do. If we can find a guitar, I'll teach them a few Christmas songs." He favored Unity with an appreciative glance. "This is a great idea, Unity. I don't mind admitting that being away from my parents during this holiday season has made me homesick. I keep remembering the pond in back of our house and the skating parties we had in December and January."

"Yes, I know. Although I don't particularly like cold weather, during these days of incessant rain, and mud, mud, mud, I've longed for a deep, white New England snow." Unity didn't mention the part that hurt most of all. This year Levi would be big enough for some toys, and she wouldn't be there to see his pleasure.

Unity went into the warehouse to determine how they could rearrange the crates and barrels to accommodate their Chinese friends. Her thoughts turned to a gift for Matt, and she looked at the bolts of fabric, but she had little choice. She was tired of the red calico that so many miners wore. Unity fingered some white silk, thinking he might like a new shirt. True, she'd never seen Matt dressed up, but if they married this year, he could use a silk shirt. Unity's face grew warm. *Had* she decided to marry him? Could the solutions to her problem come this year?

Before she had time to answer her own questions, Unity snipped off several yards of the white silk. Perhaps if she and Jiang worked together, they could finish the shirt before Christmas. For Sid she took enough red calico for a shirt; that would suit his taste better than silk.

Alex and Unity planned the pageant and feast for Christmas Eve. On the twenty-third, Matt and two of the Chinese men went into the hills in back of San Francisco and returned with a pine tree. Using snippets of the red and white fabric left from the two shirts, Wang and Jiang helped Unity thread the cloth on strings, which they draped over the tree. Then they filled dozens of packets with fruit and pieces of chocolate.

"I hope there's enough for everyone," Unity worried to Jiang. After the goodies were sacked, they still had a problem. Where could they store their treats without having them raided by the rats that inhabited San Francisco? Alex came to the rescue by putting the packets in his room, where he would guard them until time for the party.

"I've been using these rats for target practice, and they don't come near my room."

On Christmas Eve, excited Chinese gathered in the warehouse, chattering in their native language. The talking ceased when Alex grouped a few of their countrymen around him to start the program.

In other circumstances, she might have laughed at the beloved hymns sung in monotone pidgin English, but tears misted Unity's eyes and her throat tightened when she heard the familiar strains of:

O come, all ye faithful, joyful and triumphant,
Come ye, O come ye to Bethlehem;
Come and behold Him, born the King of angels;
O come let us adore Him. . . .

Dimly she caught Matt's compassionate glance across the room, and she knew he comprehended her melancholy, although he could hardly understand the full reason. Last year she'd stood in her childhood home and listened to the carolers, never thinking that another Christmas would find her thousands of miles away.

Roused by a commotion at the door, she watched in amazement as dozens of burly miners crowded into the room. Unity's heart thudded. Had the men come to break up their gathering? The first ones to walk through the door looked around curiously. Matt motioned the Chinese to make room for the newcomers, who settled peacefully around the walls, and the program turned into a true Sino-Anglo celebration of Christ's birth.

How Alex had managed to teach his protégés so many songs foreign to them, Unity didn't know, but she shook off her sadness and listened to their rendition of "The First Noel," "Silent Night," and "Away in a Manger." After the first few verses, many of the miners joined in the singing, and as their tenor and bass complemented the voices of the Chinese, Unity prayed that their coming together might spell the end of some of the troubles between the two races. Perhaps the other Americans would understand, as she and Matt did, that the Chinese could contribute much to this new territory.

The fifteen-minute Christmas story was pantomimed by the Chinese while Unity read the biblical accounts from Luke and Matthew. When the shepherds kneeled to pay homage to the Christ child, Unity glanced quickly around the room. Enlightenment dawned on a few of the faces before her as some of the Chinese at last gained an understanding of God's gift to the world. It was only a beginning, but Unity envisioned the foundation of a Chinese Christian church in the Golden Gate City.

With the extra visitors, Unity knew their food wouldn't go far, but she invited everyone to share what they had provided. When it came time to distribute the gifts under the tree, she had to ask those who received a packet to share with those who had none. Unashamed tears ran down the bearded cheeks of many miners when they received a gift.

It was past midnight when all the food was consumed and Unity shouted, "Merry Christmas" to indicate that the party was over. One miner started singing, "Joy to the world! the Lord is come . . . ." Other voices joined his, and the strains of the carol surrounded them as their footsteps receded toward the town.

Matt and Sid helped clean the warehouse, and the two walked with Unity when she left the Spencer office. At the houseboat, she said, "Come in for a minute. I have Christmas gifts for each of you."

Bashfully, Sid accepted his gift. "Thanks, Miss Unity. Nobody's given me a gift for a long time. Never did get much, except some hoarhound candy and an orange."

After Sid left, Matt drew Unity toward the davenport and sat down, with his arm around her shoulders.

"It's a beautiful shirt, Unity, and I'd like to wear it on my wedding day." He reached in his pocket and handed her a packet containing a gold ring set with rubies.

When she raised questioning eyes to his, for there were no jewelry stores in San Francisco, he said, "I found it in a pawn shop. I suppose some poor miner had to sacrifice it for the necessities. I hated to take advantage of another's misfortune, but will you wear it as my wife?"

The time for decision had come. It wasn't fair to keep avoiding Matt's proposal. Suddenly, all the bitterness of her unhappy marriage to Samuel and the loss of her child overwhelmed Unity. What if she should lose Matt, too? Didn't she deserve some happiness? Slyly her conscience prodded, *But will you have any happiness when you're starting a marriage based on deceit?* Should she make a clean breast of her past and then see if Matt still wanted to marry her? Unity rejected that idea at once. What if he'd walk off and leave her? She'd be so alone.

Quickly, as if to stall her conscience, she said, "Yes, Matt, I'll marry you."

In spite of her misgivings, it was bound to come out all right, Unity thought as she reveled in the passion of Matt's caresses. His tenderness erased forever the humiliation she'd endured at the hands of Samuel. She returned kiss for kiss, ardor for ardor, until breathlessly she removed herself from his arms.

"I don't want to wait much longer, Unity. When?"

"Oh, Matt. I just don't know. Things are so uncertain. Let's not set a date yet. Why couldn't we go to Uncle John's for the ceremony? I'd want him to be present, and the surroundings at the ranch are so much better than here. The warehouse was all right for the Christmas party, but I'd hate to be married there. Let's see what Uncle John says."

Nibbling provokingly on her ear, Matt laughed softly. "That's a good idea. I'm sure John will throw quite a party for us, if he has the chance. But I wish it could be soon." One look at her face, and he fell silent.

After Matt's departure, while she prepared for bed, Unity's conscience attacked her again: *You should tell him*. She tried to shove the thought out of her mind, determined that nothing was going to interfere with what might be her last chance for happiness. It was a long time before she slept.

Christmas Day dawned sunny, and after dinner with Sid and the Soongs, Unity and Matt toured the streets of San Francisco. Thousands of people jostled them as they sought dry footing. Only a few of the streets had sidewalks, and in some places they sank to their ankles in the mire. Mudholes were everywhere, and Matt and Unity laughed at a sign beside one deep puddle, THROUGH PASSAGE TO CHINA.

Two horseback riders plodded down the middle of the street, and in places the horses floundered to their knees. Dozens of saloons enjoyed a flourishing business, and gambling houses were set up in tents and hastily constructed buildings. Unity lowered her eyes when they passed the Golden Palace, for several scantily clad girls peered from the window. She saw the come-hither looks they threw at Matt, and her face burned.

"The whole town is a den of iniquity, if I've ever seen one," Matt commented when they again reached the comfort of her houseboat. "I shudder when I think what it will be like in another year. When shiploads of people from all over the world start arriving, this town will explode."

"Perhaps the government won't be far behind with some law and order."

"In the meantime, I hope you'll find a gun and learn to use it." He looked at her skeptically. "I don't suppose there's any use for me to ask you to marry me right away and travel with me on the boat."

She shook her head. "I'm responsible for Spencer Shipping. I feel guilty even staying here and marrying, rather than going back East to help my sister with the business. How could I leave her with this on top of it?"

"Can't she carry on that end of the enterprise, if you're doing the same out here?"

"No. Margaret and I aren't alike. My father taught me how to operate the business. Since he had no sons, he thought one of us should know the shipping industry. Margaret wasn't interested, so it was up to me."

A few days after the Christmas celebration, Lin approached Alex and Unity at the office.

"Good idea, Christmas party. Chinese want to pay back. Observe New Year our way."

Unity nodded. "We would like that. When is the Chinese New Year?"

"Sometime in January or February in old country, but we celebrate next week, maybe."

"That will be fine, for soon Matt and I will need to visit my uncle's rancho to make wedding plans. Tell us about the celebration."

"Long time ago, Chinese used lions to expel demons. Do that in our dance. Set off firecrackers to scare away bad-luck spirits."

"We'll look forward to it."

The news spread about the Chinese parade, and most of the residents of San Francisco must have lined the wharf area to watch. Many Chinese, covered with cloth to resemble a dragon, pirouetted down the boardwalk. Firecrackers exploded, dropping scraps of paper on the spectators. A masked performer teased a painted, paper lion, which bowed, shook its head, rolled its eyes, and charged the performer in pretended rage. The whole parade marched to a drum Lin had made from some old lumber and a steer's hide.

At the warehouse, Jiang and Wang served small pastry rolls filled with a mixture of meat, cabbage, onion, garlic, and salt. The roll was served with a spicy sauce and hot tea. The food was gone long before the last miner filed through the line, and many turned away in disappointment.

The day after the Chinese celebration, Unity wrote to her uncle, asking for his help in her marriage. In a few days her messenger returned with John's best wishes and an invitation. He nearly commanded them to visit immediately and celebrate the engagement, adding that he intended to invite the Swishers, from Monterey, to share in the celebration. To forestall objection, he had sent a cart along to transport any people or luggage that they wanted to bring with them.

"I'm sorry I can't take you, Alex," Unity told her trusted employee, "but I do need you here. As soon as we return, I'm sending you off to the ranch for a long vacation. Maybe you'll find a Spanish senorita to please you."

Alex smiled, and Unity marveled at the change in the boy since he'd arrived. His health had improved, and the responsibility she'd entrusted to him had matured Alex. Because of his illness, she suspected his parents had always pampered him. In San Francisco he'd become a man.

"I find that my attentions are directed elsewhere, Unity."

Lifting her eyebrows, she pondered. "Wang?" she guessed, and he nodded, eyes smiling.

"Then maybe you can go to the ranch for your wedding journey."

"Not quite that soon; I haven't asked the bride yet."

"I'm pleased for you, Alex. She's a fine girl."

He flushed at her praise. "I don't suppose my parents will approve if I marry a foreigner."

"I made one marriage to please my father, and it was a

disaster. You have the right to choose the person you want to marry, just as I'm doing now."

"I want to wish you and Matt much happiness."

Turning from Alex, Unity sighed. In spite of her resolve, she still wondered if they should marry. It wasn't only her own problems, but sometimes she suspected that Matt, too, was questioning the wisdom of their marriage. Would she someday have to choose between her son and her happiness? Hurriedly Unity turned her thoughts to business.

7

*F*og swirled around the *Allegheny*, and Matt peered through the haze, toward Unity's houseboat. He'd been sitting in the pilothouse more than an hour before he saw a light in her bedroom. Soon they'd be on their way to the ranch, and perhaps shortly he'd be a married man. After so many years as a bachelor, how would he react to having a wife?

Head in his hands, he squirmed in his chair, unaware of Sid's presence until his friend said, "Here, Matt, take a tin of coffee."

Matt grabbed the tin gratefully and took a full swallow of the hot liquid.

"Having second thoughts, boss?" Sid said with a guffaw.

"I guess so. Maybe I've lived alone too long."

"It's still not too late to call it off, but I'll bet there's a thousand men in San Francisco who'd change places with you. Do you realize how few white women there are in this territory?"

"I'm not going to call it off," Matt said testily. He set the empty tin aside and walked restlessly around the small room. "Never before have I seen a woman I've even considered marrying, so I know my love is real enough. But I don't know what kind of husband I'll make. I also couldn't sleep last night when I realized how little I know about Unity."

"You've known her for almost a year, haven't you? And as much as you've seen her, I'd think you know enough. As women go, I don't think you could do any better."

"It's what I don't know about her that's bothering me. Did you know she's been married before?"

Sid's mouth gaped in amazement. "Why, no, I didn't know that."

"That's what I mean. It's as though her past were a blank book. She rarely mentions her family or anything about her life before she left the East, as if she's drawn a curtain over a former life."

"But what does it matter? It's what she is now that should concern you."

"I used to think the world of my mother, but she showed me how false a woman can be. It took years for me to trust women again. When I met Unity, I forgot all about that, but if I found out she was like my mother, it would kill me."

Sid clapped Matt on the shoulder. "Snap out of it, Matt. You're as nervous as an old maid before her wedding night. Let me tell you, a woman isn't a goddess you can put on a pedestal and worship. Women are human, with weaknesses like the rest of us, and you're going to find that out before many more weeks. She may have some faults, but so do you."

In spite of Sid's pep talk, Matt still couldn't shake his depression, but he made up his mind that he wouldn't let Unity know how he felt. He'd been trying for months to persuade her to marry him, and he wasn't going to play the idiot now.

A crowd of Chinese gathered in front of the houseboat to speed the couple on their way. A young Mexican vaquero held the reins of a horse hitched to the cart that John had sent from the rancho. Twitching with fright, Jiang crawled into the cart, and Lin piled trunks and other baggage around her.

Sensing her fright, Unity said, "Jiang, you don't have to go if you'd prefer to stay here. I thought you wanted to help me with my wedding plans."

Jiang nodded her head stolidly. "Do. Do. Afraid to ride in cart."

"Would you rather ride a horse?"

Jiang raised her eyes, as if she implored all the gods in the Chinese pantheon. "No. No."

"I can't understand why a woman who'd come across the Pacific in a worm-eaten junk would fear to ride in a cart, but we all have our peculiarities." Glancing at Matt, Unity said, "I'm ready."

He helped her into the saddle of the horse John had sent for her use, mounted his own, and started away from the wharf. A rousing applause rose around them, and Unity's eyes misted at the warmth of their friends' goodwill.

Near the end of the next day, red and yellow sunset rays darted across the blue sky, and Matt and Unity paused on a high promontory to watch the sun dip out of sight beyond the ocean waves. The cart passed by them, and when it was out of view, Matt dismounted and reached for Unity. He folded her in his arms.

The lonely days when he'd traveled the Ohio River, the trauma he'd experienced during the perilous wagon trip across the continent, and the frustration of the last four, ineffectual years in Oregon, were about to end. He wondered if Unity held similar emotions. She'd admitted that she hadn't loved her husband. Could their marriage help her to forget any unpleasantness of the past?

"Let's walk down to the ocean," he said. "We're not far from the ranch, so we can be there before dark." Leading their horses, they walked carefully down the shaly slope.

Hand in hand they strolled along the wet sand, and foaming, briny waves lapped around their feet as the tides receded.

The tides of time wash over my soul, scattering doubt and fear, Unity thought.

"We'll soon be starting a new life," Matt interrupted her musings. "Such a thought is as overwhelming as these ocean tides swirling around us."

"The tide has left lots of shells and seaweed on the shore. When it comes back, it'll carry all of that away. I hope that's what marriage will do for us, wash away any problems we have."

"Do you have problems in the past that you want washed away?" he questioned nonchalantly.

Unity glanced at his sober face. "It's too late to reminisce now, Matt. I haven't asked you questions about your past, nor you of mine. Let's consider that our lives entered a new phase when we met and go on from there."

Matt hoped she was right as he pulled her again into his arms. While the ebbing tide receded farther and farther from their feet, they drew strength from the love and caresses they shared there on the shores of the Pacific.

Loretta and Calvin Swisher sat with John on the patio when Matt and Unity rode into the courtyard at dusk.

Serving men and women came from all directions to take charge of horses and to help the guests dismount. John bounded down the steps and hugged Unity.

"We were about ready to send out a search party for you," he shouted.

"We weren't lost, John. I knew I'd have to share her with the rest of you for several days. We wanted a few minutes alone."

"You're a smart man," John said, pounding Matt on the back.

"So you two have decided to marry. I'm not surprised. I told Calvin, when we were crossing Panama, that you'd make a good match," Loretta said.

"It took you long enough to decide," Calvin commented in his dour manner. "We needed an excuse to see each other," he added, as if in explanation of their presence.

"We'll be eating shortly, so you two should freshen up," John said. He clapped his hands, and two native women appeared beside Unity and urged her toward the bedroom ell. "What have you done with Jiang?" Unity called as she went down the hallway.

"In a room adjacent to yours."

The maids guided her into the same room she'd had the last time she visited the rancho, where Jiang sat listlessly on a chair.

"All right, my friend?" Unity questioned.

"Tired. Tired."

"I'll ask the maids to bring some food to your room, and you lie down as soon as you've eaten. These girls will take care of my needs tonight. Then you can help me tomorrow."

She patted Jiang's shoulder and urged her into the room. Unity had picked up a few words of Spanish during the past few months, and she could at least give directions to the maids. One hurried down the hallway to bring Jiang's food, while the other prepared Unity's bath water. Unity would have liked to soak until the water lost its heat, but she knew that the evening meal would be served soon. After changing into a brown woolen dress she'd brought from Boston, Unity went toward the dining area, reaching the room just as the gong sounded and Stephano Alvarado entered.

A Spanish guitarist, seated in one corner of the room, played softly as they ate, and Loretta sighed with approval. "Now this is more what I expected California to be like. Pleasant dining, soft music, servants catering to your every whim."

"You haven't found Monterey to be like that?" Unity asked.

"Much of the time we don't even have domestic help, and Calvin doesn't care for *my* cooking. More than half of the soldiers have deserted and gone to the gold fields. At present we have a Mexican and his wife to serve us, but we don't live in luxury like this."

"You came a few years late to California," John said sympathetically. "Many natives lived like this when I came ten years ago. It was a carefree, beautiful way of life, and I embraced it. We Americans have a tendency to destroy existing cultures when we move in. That's what we did to the Indians, and it's happening now to the Mexicans."

"Isn't what we substitute superior?" Calvin asked.

"Not if you consider what San Francisco is like now," Matt answered. "When I brought my first shipload of produce from Oregon, Yerba Buena was a sleepy little town that only stirred to life when a ship entered the harbor. The Mexican garrison in the fort had so little to do that they'd shoot off a cannon occasionally just to cure their boredom, but now—"

"Say, people," Unity interrupted, "we're here to plan a wedding, remember? You sound more like you're attending a funeral."

John laughed loudly. "Guess you're right at that, niece. The old California is dead, all right, but we'll postpone the funeral. Let's be merry tonight."

He clapped his hands three times, and four festively robed dancers entered the room. Bowing deeply and shaking castanets, they swung into rollicking dance steps following the rapid tempo of the guitarist. Before they finished their performance, the guitarist slowed the pace, knelt beside Unity, and sang in lilting, soft Spanish what she supposed must be a native love song. While he sang, the four dancers swayed to the mild rhythm of the music, reminding Unity of the ocean waves she and Matt had watched during the afternoon.

Unity missed the briny smell from the harbor and the noisy stamping feet of prospective miners, when she awakened the next morning to the sound of sea gulls noisily invading the cooking area, where the natives were preparing breakfast. The smell of freshly baked bread wafted in through the closed shutters, and she supposed the cooks were removing the loaves from the oval earthen ovens.

Wrapping a robe around her nightdress, she stepped out on the patio and looked toward the rear courtyard, where they worked.

A Mexican maid appeared at her door with hot water, and Unity sent the girl for some tea and tortillas. When she had eaten, Unity admitted Jiang into her room, and together they began tentative wedding plans. Though they had no date set, the couple would still need a guest list, plans for food to be brought in from San Francisco, and the number of cattle necessary to feed a hungry crowd.

Already Unity had found the material for her wedding dress; she and Jiang would spend hours working on it together, and when she'd unearthed the material in her warehouse, she felt it was wise to take it. Would Matt like the voluminous-skirted, rose-silk gown? Would he even notice it? Suddenly realizing how fully she'd committed herself to a course of action that filled her with doubts, Unity knew she could not rush into anything. Yet what would become of her love for Matt?

The muted sounds of the rancho awakened Matt, and he slowly opened his eyelids. He couldn't imagine where he was at first, until he identified the sounds related to cattle: the blacksmith's tools, the occasional lowing of a steer, and hooves hitting packed earth.

Yesterday's ride had been heavenly. If only they could marry right away. Yet Unity had hesitated whenever he tried to settle the marriage quickly, and he wondered why.

That morning Unity explained gently that she thought they'd better wait until the fall to marry.

"You're trying to say you don't want to marry me, aren't you?" A hurt look crossed Matt's face. "Perhaps you don't love me enough to put Whitley behind you?"

"No, Matt, it's not that. You know I love you as I never did that man!"

"Did he hurt you so much that you'll never trust me?" Matt's anger burned hot against the man who could have caused her such pain.

"Samuel Whitley was horrible, but I don't confuse him with you, Matt. I know you'd never harm me so." She turned away to hide her tears. "I just don't feel this is God's timing. I need more time. . . ." Even in her own ears the excuse sounded feeble, but Matt did not seek to change her mind.

"Let's discuss our plans with John anyway, for this summer will be busy for me," Matt said. "We probably won't have an opportunity to come here again."

"Loretta says they know the priest at Carmel Mission, and she will take a letter to him about performing the ceremony."

During the rest of the day they discussed plans with John and the Swishers.

"We'll want you and Calvin to stand up with us," Unity said to Loretta.

"Do you want a real Spanish wedding?" John asked. "When Maria and I were married, I think the celebration must have lasted for a month. We feasted, danced, watched horse races, enjoyed guitar music, and visited."

"Sounds like a good idea to me," Loretta said. "I find a lot of time on my hands."

"I'll invite all our neighbors," John continued, "and you bring anyone you want from San Francisco. But I'll need at least a month's notice, so you let me know as soon as you set the date."

At dinner that evening, Matt announced, "Since everything is all planned, we might as well leave tomorrow."

Surely he had not traveled all this way to return so quickly, the Swishers objected. What of Unity? At their insistence, the engaged couple planned to accompany them to Monterey for a short visit.

"You know that once you're married and Matt's on his steamboat runs, he won't take time for a visit. You're close by now, so please stay for a few days," Loretta insisted. "With a fall wedding, you've got no need to rush."

"The trail from Monterey to San Francisco is almost impassable this time of year," John warned.

"Ships stop by often on their way northward; you could probably continue your journey by sea," Calvin suggested to Matt.

So they sent Jiang back to San Francisco, escorted by a vaquero and his wife, and Matt and Unity set out for Monterey with the Swishers. Unity looked forward to seeing the old Spanish capital, but reflecting on the visit in years to come, she could remember little except the trip to Monterey had resulted in one of the most shattering events of her life.

As they neared the city, they stopped for a view of Carmel Mission, which dominated a slope above the river and bay. The sandstone used in the construction had been quarried in the nearby hills, and Unity admired the grandeur of the architecture.

"There's the custom house where Commodore Sloat first raised the Stars and Stripes, when the United States claimed California," Calvin commented, pointing to a long structure with a central wing and balconied towers on each end.

Calvin explained that Monterey's early residents had lived inside the Spanish-built presidio, but Unity noticed that there were now many houses on the grassy plain extending from the fort to the nearby hills.

Loretta pointed toward another house, built of sandstone and adobe bricks, which resembled a southern plantation.

"That was built by Thomas O. Larkin, when he came here fifteen years ago."

"After San Francisco, this village is spectacular," Unity said. "Compared to the tents and shacks we see day after day, these buildings look like mansions."

Before they arrived at the Swishers' quarters, Matt noticed a ship in the harbor. "I'm going to check on that ship, and see what direction it's heading. I'll be along soon."

Finding that the vessel was heading toward San Francisco, Matt booked passage to travel on it.

"We'll need to leave day after tomorrow," he told Loretta, who received the news with a pout.

"I had hoped for a week or more."

"I'm sorry, but I must return as soon as possible, and if we don't take this ship, I don't know when another may come."

"At least you must meet some of the other military men here. I'll plan a tea tomorrow afternoon. Calvin, please issue the invitations."

Unity became aware of the large, florid man the moment he entered the Swishers' home the next day, but it was more than an hour before she finally identified the man behind the snub nose and bushy eyebrows. Obsessed with the idea that she knew him, she couldn't stop looking his way, and too frequently their glances met.

When she noticed the twitching left eye, Unity staggered and almost dropped the bowl of tea she held. Suddenly her mind reeled backward, when in the midst of the most painful night of her life, she had sensed the presence of that twitching eye.

I have to leave here, she moaned inwardly, but Loretta barred her way, steered her toward the man with the twitching eye, and introduced them. "Miss Unity Spencer, I don't believe you've met our post doctor, Micah Dilcher. He's from Massachusetts, so perhaps you've met him before."

Unity shook her head; her throat was too dry to utter a sound. Loretta moved away, and Unity wanted to shout, *Don't leave me alone with this man!*

"Unity," Dilcher commented. "A most unusual name. A few years ago I attended a woman in childbirth, who had that name. Strange how much she looked like you."

"Surely you can remember your patients better than that," she said, trying to affect a teasing manner.

"The house I went to belonged to the Smiths, but the owner married into the Spencer family. Could it have been a relative?"

"If you'll excuse me, Dr. Dilcher, I must speak to my betrothed. Nice to have met you."

Unity moved away on trembling legs, numbness flooding her mind. Why had she ever tried to deceive Matt? Why hadn't she told him about Levi? *I felt safe, thousands of miles from Boston, and only wanted to save Matt heartache by never telling him, she told herself.* But her mind would not stop there. *Had* she really wanted to spare him pain, or had she simply feared losing the man she loved?

Turning once, she met Dilcher's cold, calculating stare, and she knew it would be a matter of time before Matt knew the worst about her.

Reaching her room, Unity collapsed on the bed, and she fell across the Bible she'd been reading earlier in the day. She moved the Book to the table beside the bed, remembering the promise "God is our refuge and strength, a very present help in trouble."

She believed those words with all her heart, but what if one's own actions had brought on the trouble? She needed God's help desperately, but how could she ask for His guidance when she'd not heeded the promptings of her conscience? She deserved to suffer. Why hadn't she been honest with Matt?

8

The first wave of prospectors from the States arrived on February twenty-eighth, when the steamship *California* entered the Golden Gate, carrying over four hundred passengers. Matt and Unity mingled with the crowd waiting at the dock to welcome the first steamship to complete the trip around Cape Horn since news of the gold strike had reached the East. In honor of the arrival, the commander of the Pacific Squadron of the United States Navy, at anchor in San Francisco, ordered a thunderous salute to greet the ship. Passengers leaned over the rail and cheered, waving to those on the land.

"That's twice as many people as that boat should carry," Sid Green commented to Matt.

"It's a miracle the vessel made it at all, loaded like that."

Unity peered closely at the faces of the newcomers to see if any of them might be from New England, and who might recognize her. She hadn't yet gotten over the shock of seeing Micah Dilcher in Monterey and lived in fear that the man would manage to reveal her past to Matt.

Sid stayed behind at the wharf after Unity and Matt returned to her houseboat. Later he pecked on the door. "Come in, Sid," Unity greeted. "Stay for supper with us. Jiang has been cooking all afternoon. We might as well celebrate the arrival of the new residents. You and Matt will have plenty of passengers when you start upriver."

"I talked to one of the *California's* crewmen and learned a lot. We'd better hold a wake, rather than a celebration. According to that sailor, this is just a small beginning of what's to come. He said the gold rush didn't receive much notice back East until President Polk made the news official in his annual message to Congress in December. After that, the population went crazy."

"Everybody wanting to get rich quick, I guess," Matt commented.

"The *California* has been sent here to run the mail service between California and Panama. Prior to Polk's message, she had been scheduled to depart. Before that, the factories had already stepped up production of picks, shovels, boots, and other mining gear. Pawnshops overflow with jewelry, silverware, watches, and other possessions. Men are mortgaging their homes and leaving their families without provision, to run to the gold fields!"

"But is there gold for so many, Matt?"

"No," he thundered. "Last fall Sutter told me that easily found gold is already scarce. In less than a year most of these people will be looking for passage back home, and they'll go with empty pockets."

"The sailor said that only those with some money are coming by sea. The poorer people plan to travel overland. He'd picked up an old New York newspaper in Panama. The government estimates that more than twenty thousand people will travel over the Oregon Trail this year."

Matt groaned. "And they'll know they've had a jaunt, too. I'm not sorry I had the experience of that overland journey, but it's one I don't want to repeat."

As Unity helped Jiang place the food on the table, she fretted about the influx of easterners. It was quite likely that they'd have hundreds of argonauts from Boston, and no doubt some of them would know her. Would one of them tell Matt about her past life? Could someone know that Levi was her son?

After Sid left, she snuggled into Matt's arms. In two days he'd be gone again, and she'd feel empty inside until his return.

"Unity," he said musingly, "I've been thinking of building a residence. A few houses are going up on the hills in back of town, and with this invasion of emigrants, land will soon be scarce and expensive. I'm making lots of money, and I'd like to use it to build a house for you. Would you like that?"

"I'm quite happy here in the houseboat, but if we should have a family, we'd be very crowded. I want a family. Don't you, Matt?"

His arms tightened. "I can hardly comprehend what it would be like to have a child of my own, but yes, I'd like it."

"Then, by all means, let's build a house. When our family arrives, we'll be ready."

Unity felt almost desperate to have a baby, for even yet she could remember the soft form of Levi as Deborah placed him in her arms for the first time. Remembering the child's birth reminded her of Dr. Dilcher. Had he told the Swishers what he knew about her?

Dreading another encounter with Dilcher or anyone else who might know her, Unity looked with suspicion on all visitors, and early in April, she was startled when a beautiful blond woman and a dark-haired man carrying a child entered the office.

"Are you Unity Spencer?" the woman asked in soft, modulated tones.

Hesitantly, Unity answered, "Why, yes, I am."

"I'm Becky, Matt Miller's sister, and this is my husband, Maurie."

Unity circled the desk and extended her arms to Becky. "Matt told me he'd written you about our betrothal. I'm so pleased to meet you. Sit down."

She moved papers from a bench, motioned for them to sit, and reached for the boy, who readily came into her arms. "Who is this?"

"This is David," Maurie answered.

After a close inspection of Unity, the child reached for his mother, and Unity released him reluctantly.

"Matt's message that he planned to marry surprised us almost as much as when we learned he'd found gold, but we're greatly pleased that he found both you and the gold," Matt's sister said.

"We thought Matt was a confirmed bachelor," Maurie said with a laugh, "which goes to show we never know what's in another's head."

"I remember he told me once that he wished he had someone who would love him as much as I love you," Becky said, with a fond glance at her husband. Swinging her gaze to Unity, she added, "I hope you do."

"Well, I love him a great deal." Alex entered the office then, and Unity said, "Alex, Matt's relatives have come to visit. If you can handle things the rest of the day, I'll take them to the houseboat."

As they walked toward the harbor, Unity asked, "What

brings you to California? Are you looking for gold, Maurie?"

"Not the kind I have to dig for. I brought a load of cattle down here, and I had buyers climbing up on the boat, begging for them, before we even landed. They started auctioning between themselves, and by the time the ship's anchor dropped, I'd gotten so much money for those cattle that I thought I'd struck gold. I'd intended to take them to the gold fields, but this was a good market."

"You'd probably have made more profit up the river, but if you're like Matt and me, we don't try to fleece people, just ask for a reasonable rate. Though what you'd call reasonable here wouldn't be that elsewhere."

"With all the cattle in California, I didn't suppose the demand would be so great."

"California beef is tough, not grain-fed, like yours."

"But I came to meet you, Unity," Becky said. "We'll be adding another member to our family in November, and we can't attend your wedding. I wanted to see you and Matt before I need to start staying home."

"Matt isn't here now, but I expect him within the next few days."

Unity could scarcely keep her hands off David, and before bedtime, he'd accepted her. She'd given up her bed to Becky and Maurie, and she wanted to ask if David could sleep with her on the sofa, but knowing she shouldn't arouse any suspicion in their minds, she gave the child unwillingly into his mother's arms.

Two days later, when, with black smoke rolling and the paddle wheels churning water, Matt pulled into the dock, Maurie and Becky stood beside Unity, waiting for him. Outside influences never distracted Matt, when he was landing his steamboat, so he didn't see the group until his crew had the boat tied securely.

Recognition didn't come at once, but suddenly he gave a shout, and raced across the gangplank. "Sister," he cried, and enveloped Becky in a bear hug. Extending his hand to Maurie, he pounded him on the shoulder. "More than a year since I've seen you. Have you come to stay?"

Maurie's laugh was carefree. "There's not enough gold in the world to tempt me to live in this circus. I walked around town last night, and I counted more than thirty saloons, twenty or so gambling houses, and several other buildings of a questionable nature. Besides, it's the dirtiest city I've ever been in. Dogs were chasing hordes of rats, and people jostled against one another on the streets until you could scarcely walk. I can't believe that you like it here, Matt."

"I'm not in San Francisco much, and when I am, I stay on the boat."

"It's no better down here at the harbor. Two United States ships docked today, overloaded with passengers, and I've counted several vessels flying European flags. Newly arrived ships can hardly find a place to dock."

"Obviously you don't like our home," Unity said, "but you're here now, so we can have a good visit. Matt will be in port a few days."

After supper, Matt said, "I've had an idea circulating around in my head, Maurie. Why can't all of you go with me on my next run to the gold region? Unity hasn't gone with me, and this is a good chance."

"Do you have room for all of us?" Unity said. "I can wait and go later, and Becky and Maurie can have your cabin."

"If need be, Sid won't mind giving up his. You can surely leave for a few days."

"Yes, Alex can handle everything. We had a ship come in last week with provisions, but we've unloaded and tallied those. The captain has already started his return voyage. I can make the journey if the rest want to."

"I might as well see what's going on. How long will it take?" Maurie said.

"I'm running between San Francisco and Sacramento City in about three days now. I usually lay over a bit, but we can have you back in less than ten days."

"The owner of the sloop that brought my cattle was heading down to Monterey, perhaps even to Los Angeles, so that will be several days before he returns. We'll go, if Becky feels up to it."

Noting Becky's expression as she nodded her agreement, Unity deduced that Maurie's wishes were always what Becky wanted. Would she ever be such a dutiful and devoted wife? Could Matt ever be satisfied with anything less?

Unity had to admit that she'd been jealous of Becky, because she thought that Matt compared every move she made to what his sister would have done; but on the journey up the Sacramento River, Unity realized that Becky *was* a wonderful person. She loved David and gave him constant attention, although she soon corrected him if the boy got out of line. The love between her and Maurie was so obvious, when their glances caught and held, that pain pierced Unity's heart. Why did her relationship with Matt have to be strained because of the hidden secrets in her past? Now she felt the heavy price they exacted from her soul.

Since the *Allegheny* was crowded with passengers, Unity and Becky spent much of their time in Matt's cabin. One day, after the men left them and while Unity held the sleeping David on her lap, Becky began quietly, "Unity, how much has Matt told you about our past?"

Suddenly it dawned upon Unity that she didn't know

any more about Matt's youth than he knew about *her* life in the East.

"Very little."

"I imagined so, and I think you should know some of the things that make Matt the way he is. Although he's changed quite a lot since we came to Oregon, he can still be stubborn at times."

"We haven't had any problems."

"Maybe not, but if you should, I want you to know that the way hasn't always been smooth for Matt nor for Maurie and me."

"You're so much in love now that it's hard to believe you've had problems."

"My mother died when I was young, and Matt took on the responsibility of raising me. He found that quite a chore, for men seemed to pursue me, and since my mother hadn't been married to my father, Matt feared the same thing would happen to me. He guarded me constantly, and I resented it."

"What about your father?"

"He abandoned my mother before I was born. Matt worshiped Mother, and it was years before he forgave her for the indiscretion of my birth. A man tried to assault me on the riverboat one night, and I shot him, so Matt made up his mind to move to Oregon for my protection."

"You killed him?"

"No, but I didn't know that I hadn't until we arrived in Oregon and found the man there very much alive. Maurie was the guide of our wagon train, and we fell in love right away. Maurie was already married, although he had a legal divorce from his wife, who was in a mental asylum. We were free to marry, but Matt has strong ideas about divorce, and didn't think Maurie had any right to marry when he had a living wife. After we got to Oregon, we discovered Maurie's wife had died months before, but I tell you there were many unhappy days before we had that news."

Before this revelation, Unity had considered confiding in Becky about her marriage to Samuel and the birth of Levi, to see if Becky thought she should reveal everything to Matt. The answer was obvious now—if Matt ever learned she had deceived him, she'd topple off the pedestal where he'd placed her. Fear of losing him clutched her heart.

They passed Sutter's Fort on the early morning of their third day out of San Francisco. Maurie, Becky, and Unity stood in the small pilothouse with Matt as he pointed out the landmarks.

"We used to tie up at the fort, but since Sacramento City started a few months ago, that's the center of business. I feel sorry for Sutter. He's lost about everything."

As the city came into view Maurie said, "But if this city was established on Sutter's land, seems as if he should have been paid for it."

"A few paid for their land, but most seized his property and sold it to others. Sutter has tried to have his claims recognized by United States officials, but none of them will take a stand."

Considering that the town had only been organized around the first of the year, Sacramento City boasted some fairly large buildings, most of which were made of lumber, although one three-storied brick building fronted the harbor. A wide, dirt street led uphill from the river's edge. The town looked barren, for most of the vegetation was gone, with the exception of a few oak trees scattered along the muddy streets.

"There's a hotel, and we'll take lodging there if we can,

for I want to take Maurie up to the diggings. You women will be more comfortable in a hotel while we're gone."

Unity felt like a horse with two heads as they walked from the *Allegheny* to the hotel; she suffered the stares of the many men lounging along the street.

"Why are they so rude?" she demanded of Matt.

"They probably haven't seen a woman for months, and then to have two who look like you and Becky show up, it's too much for them."

One whiskered miner, resplendent in a red calico shirt, stopped in front of Unity. "Are you married, woman? I've got a good claim and thousands of dollars in gold dust."

Matt brushed him out of the way. "She's marrying me. Keep away from her."

David received as much attention as the women, and more than one miner reached out and touched him. When Becky instinctively drew the child closer, Maurie shook his head. "Let them touch the boy; these men probably left children at home."

"Whew!" Becky said when they entered the hotel. The rooms were all occupied, but when the owner realized that two women needed lodging, he bawled to his servant, "Clear out one of the rooms; the men can sleep in the hall. We have to take care of the ladies."

The interior of the building, with its dirt floors and calico-covered walls, belied the grandeur of its brick exterior. The downstairs was divided into a barroom on the left, and on the right rows of tables and chairs indicated the dining area.

At the top of a short flight of steps, Unity and Becky were shown to a small room, not more than eight by ten feet, and the one window was curtained with the ever-present red calico. A heavy wooden bed dominated the room, and the mattress appeared to be filled with grass and covered with woolen blankets. Looking at the door, nothing more than a frame covered with some black cloth, Unity knew they would have been more comfortable and probably safer on the *Allegheny*, but she didn't want to insult the proprietor, after he'd evicted other guests to make room for them.

When the man left them, Matt looked around apologetically. "I thought it would be better than this."

"It's all right, Matt, we'll manage. You and Maurie go on to the gold fields," Becky said.

"I'll take you to the theater when we return. Sid can escort you to supper tonight."

After they'd eaten their meal of beef stew and dried-apple pie, Sid said, "Want to take a tour of the town? It's still daylight."

"Matt might not like it," Becky said.

Unity noticed that it was *Matt's* opinion, not Maurie's, that concerned Becky.

Sid shrugged his shoulders, "What Matt doesn't know won't hurt him any. Besides, no one in this town will bother two decent women."

Their tour revealed hastily constructed edifices, mostly built of lumber, although they saw a few adobe buildings and even some log structures. The principal street teemed with laughing, talking, singing men. Hucksters tried to steer the miners into their gambling houses or saloons, and a few heavily painted females walked back and forth in front of brothels. One miner bawled in a loud voice,

> "My name it is Joe Bowers,
> I have a brother Ike,
> I come from old Missouri,
> Yes, all the way from Pike."

Delivering his charges back to the hotel, Sid said, "Can you understand why I prefer the decks of the *Allegheny* to life landside?"

"Yes, even San Francisco is better than this new town," Unity agreed

In a day's ride up the American River, Matt and Maurie passed dozens of tent towns. The beautiful hills Matt had admired on his first trip to the Sierras were mutilated by shafts of groundhog mines and desecrated by dirty tents erected among piles of dirt thrown up from the holes. They dismounted at one site and walked among the workers.

Some men stood knee-deep in water, using a pan to separate gold nuggets from the gravel. Others worked in teams around wooden objects, similar to the cradle Maurie had made for David. It was a wooden box mounted on rockers and open at the lower end, with a coarse sieve at its head. Wooden cleats, nailed across the bottom, caught the gold as the water filtered out of the cradle.

"This method is faster than panning," Matt said, "but it takes a team of three or more men to work the rocker, dig the dirt, and supply the buckets."

"Hard way to make money," Maurie said as he remounted.

As they rode away from the camp, Matt said, "This place could be vacated by tonight. If the miners hear there's a strike on another creek, they could fold up these tents and be gone in a hurry."

Poorly constructed boardinghouses, restaurants, saloons, gambling houses, brothels, and stores huddled together in the towns they passed. In many places, tents provided the only shelter.

Some of the miners wore eastern clothes, others deer-skin breeches and sombreros. Most, however, were dressed in red or blue flannel shirts, with woolen pants tucked into high-top boots. The garments were worn and ragged, and many of them obviously hadn't been washed for weeks.

As they rode through the streets of one town, Matt said, "This is really the place I wanted you to see. Up there on that hill is where I found my gold. Thousands of dollars have been taken from this spot. If I'd stayed here last February, I could have had most of it. Do you think I was crazy to run away from all of this wealth?"

"Don't you have everything you want?"

"Yes. I'm making a living operating a steamboat, and I have Unity."

"That's your answer, Matt. Remember the Bible says, 'But godliness with contentment is great gain. For we brought nothing into this world, and it is certain we can carry nothing out. And having food and raiment let us be therewith content.'"

Maurie looked around at the makeshift town. "Gold doesn't bring happiness, and I want to leave here before I develop a yearning to hunt for it. Let's go back to our loved ones. I've seen enough."

"I doubt that the theater will amount to much more than the hotel, but maybe it will be entertaining," Matt said as he guided his party through the streets of Sacramento City.

Inside the building, noisy miners already crowded rows of rough benches, but the four of them squeezed into seats near the stage, which consisted of several rough planks placed across logs. The curtain was made of red calico.

"I'm beginning to think there isn't any other material except red calico," Becky whispered in amusement.

"Maybe these miners just like red," Maurie said.

A few lanterns hung around the walls, but still the dim light screened the faces of the people near them. When the curtain was pulled, a woman well past middle age came onstage and sang, in a cultured voice, songs that Unity remembered from the past. Some of the songs, however, were ballads of the gold fields, and the miners joined noisily in, singing, "What was your name in the States? Was it Thompson or Johnson or Bates? Did you murder your wife and fly for your life? Say, what was your name in the States?"

Nostalgically, the miners sang with the woman, "Oh, don't you remember sweet Alice, Ben Bolt, sweet Alice, with hair so brown? She wept with delight when you gave her a smile, and trembled with fear at your frown."

How many of these men had left "Sweet Alice's" behind to seek their fortunes? Unity knew that many a "Sweet Alice" would wait in vain for the return of her lover.

The woman's husband entertained with several selections from *Macbeth*, and *Romeo and Juliet*. During intermission, the two entertainers filed up and down the aisle selling Elixir, a guaranteed cure for the rheumatism and scurvy common to the miners. This apparently was the only compensation the couple received, since no admission charge had been made for the show, so Matt and Maurie both bought a bottle of the medicine.

"Probably half water, but I suppose it's worth a dollar to see the show," Matt muttered.

To their right, a man shouted, "Don't sell all of that miracle medicine before you get over here. I'm heading to the diggings tomorrow, and I'll need some Elixir."

The familiarity of the voice caught Unity's attention, and she glanced quickly at the man. Cold chills ran down her spine, only to be replaced by a sickly warmth throughout her veins. Even in the dim light, she recognized the bulk of the man.

As soon as the performance started again, Unity whispered to Matt, "Will you take me back to the hotel? I don't feel well."

With a brief explanation to Becky, Unity hurried as inconspicuously as possible out of the theater. She had to leave this place before those miners did.

"What's the matter, Unity? I've never known you to be sick."

"I feel better now that I'm out in the air, but the smell in that little building stifled me, and I thought I was going to faint." She couldn't explain that she'd just seen a dead man.

"If you feel better, do you want to go back for the show?"

"No, no. If you'll see me to the hotel, I'll be all right, and then you can return."

Unity didn't go down for breakfast the next morning, rather she stood at the window watching the passersby. After an hour of scrutiny, she saw what she dreaded to see. She'd hoped during the sleepless hours of the night that she'd only imagined the identity of the man in the theater, but at last she saw him among a group of men on a loaded wagon, presumably bound for the diggings. It was Samuel Whitley all right, the man she thought had drowned in the Atlantic Ocean over two years ago. She was legally divorced from him, but she remembered Becky's words, "Matt . . . didn't think Maurie had any right to marry when he had a living wife."

Wife or husband—it made no difference. If Matt found out that Samuel Whitley was alive, her marriage to him was doomed. Was it right not to tell Matt? What if Samuel should find out about Levi? Biting her lip to keep back the tears, Unity leaned her head on the windowsill. *What am I going to do?*

9

Maurie and Becky left for Oregon soon after their return to San Francisco, and Matt tarried only a few days before he headed upstream again.

For the next two months San Francisco teemed with excitement as gold seekers thronged its streets. Miners, supplies, and gold poured through the Golden Gate. San Francisco changed quickly from a village of tents and shacks to a metropolis. Buzzing saws and noisy hammers could be heard day and night.

Making money by buying and selling was the order of the day, and Spencer Shipping made its share of the profit. In spite of all this activity, Unity hadn't had a peaceful minute since she'd discovered the presence of Samuel Whitley; nevertheless, she gave thanks that three thousand miles of land and many more miles of water separated Levi from his father. Unwilling, indeed unable, to assume any more trauma, Unity overlooked Jiang's mournful face while she ate her breakfast, one morning in early July, but as she lingered over a last cup of coffee, she finally said, "What's the matter, Jiang?"

"Trouble. Big trouble, missy."

Unity sighed in frustration. Sometimes it was impossible to extract information from Jiang.

"What kind of trouble?"

"One of the Hounds is after Wang."

"What!"

"Yesterday he go to hotel, grab her, and carry her away. She escape from him, but now she afraid. Won't go out. Hounds mean to Chinese. Cut off pigtails."

"I'm sorry, Jiang, but I don't know what I can do about it. Tell her not to go to work, but stay hidden. Perhaps Wang needs to find a husband to protect her," Unity added, thinking this might be the time for Alex to speak.

When she commented on it to Alex, he said, "The Hounds are becoming bolder all the time. They walk into restaurants, eat their fill, leave without paying, steal anything they want in a store, and the merchants are afraid to protest, because the Hounds threaten to wreck their establishments. But if I catch one of them bothering Wang again, I'll shoot him."

"No wonder Wang is scared. Why don't you marry the girl? She'd probably be safer if she were your wife."

"I mean to speak to Lin soon, but no one is going to be safe in this town much longer. I've heard the hoodlums are starting a campaign against the Chilenos now, so perhaps they'll leave the Chinese alone for the present."

The Hounds hadn't bothered Spencer Shipping, but the next day, while Alex and Unity were inventorying a new shipment from the East, three men walked into the warehouse. Unity paid little attention to two of them, but the third one was Micah Dilcher.

"We're in need of a few provisions, and we heard you'd

gotten a shipment of clothing," one of the men said as he grabbed an armload of shirts and trousers lying on a table, bowed to Unity, and walked out.

Dr. Dilcher's twitching eye surveyed Unity with a sneer. "What a pleasure to meet you again, Miss Spencer," he said before he left the building.

Unity gritted her teeth in frustration that she had allowed these men to steal her supplies, but the presence of Dilcher had stunned her.

Alex hurried to her side. "Do you feel all right, Unity? Sit down."

"I'm too mad to sit down. I can't believe we actually let them steal those clothes."

Alex muttered apologetically, "I didn't know what to do. We'd never discussed our procedure if the Hounds tried to plunder our stores."

"I certainly didn't want you to risk your life, Alex. I'm the one who should have protested, but it happened so rapidly that I couldn't think."

"Surprise is one of the Hounds' best tactics, it seems. Who was the second man who spoke to you?"

"I saw him in Monterey last January. He was in the army then, but I suppose he's deserted, like so many other military men."

A few days later, on July fifteenth, the Hounds made a concerted attack on the Chilenos. They started out with a parade through the main streets of San Francisco, waving banners, playing fifes and drums. They made a tour of the saloons, and if the owners seemed reluctant to give them what they demanded, they smashed bottles and mirrors. Finally, filled with liquor, they raided the slum settlement of the Chilenos, set fire to the tent city, and assaulted hundreds of other citizens.

The next morning, Sam Brannan called upon Unity. This

was the first time she'd met the man who was the acknowledged leader of the better citizens of San Francisco.

"Miss Spencer, I assume you've heard about the Hounds' attack upon the Chileno settlement yesterday."

"I could hardly have helped it," she said. "None of us slept last night, for we felt we had to guard our property. Even if the hoodlums didn't attack us personally, I don't like having a fire started in the town. As many flimsy structures as we have, San Francisco could go up in flames in a few hours."

"Exactly! And while most of us will not miss the Chilenos, it's occurred to us that if the Hounds can wreck and loot one part of the city, they'll try the same thing elsewhere. We've organized a committee of reputable citizens, and we intend to round up these scoundrels and run them out of town. I wanted to ask if you will support us."

"Certainly. Mr. Smith probably could be of assistance to you, too."

Alex nodded.

"Good. We'll have a meeting at my store tonight, and we'd like you to attend."

Within three days many of the Hounds had been apprehended by the citizens' committee and brought to trial. Several were sentenced to prison.

"We don't even have a prison," Alex said to Unity, with a laugh, when he reported on some of the trial proceedings. "So I suppose none of the culprits will be punished, but I understand the Hounds are leaving town at a fast rate. Our gain is another's loss, but we're happy to be rid of them."

The next morning Unity was in the office alone, when she looked up at the sound of footsteps. Micah Dilcher stood before her desk, and outside, on the steps, she noticed two other men.

"Good morning," he said.

Unity didn't answer him.

"My friends and I have encountered a bit of difficulty and find we must leave San Francisco. But I'm a poor man, Miss Spencer. I've heard that you have prospered. Perhaps you could make me a loan of five hundred dollars. Living is quite expensive in the gold fields."

"Dilcher, I won't give you any money. Please leave the office."

Unity tried to hold his gaze, but the twitching eye unnerved her.

"Your betrothed, Matt Miller, would probably be happy to loan me the money in exchange for the information that I have."

Every muscle in Unity's body pulsed when she considered that this man would go to Matt and that he might also encounter Samuel and tell him about the birth of her child. *Should I give him money to keep him quiet?* Her mind reeled when she remembered how angry she'd been when she hadn't stopped these people from raiding her warehouse. Five hundred dollars wouldn't last long, and if she paid him now, she knew he'd be back for more.

God, give me courage to do the right thing.

Standing, Unity slipped open a desk drawer, and she said with a laugh, "Assuming that you *do* know something about me, what makes you think that Matt doesn't already know it? If you go to him with any of these insinuations, he'll throw you in the bay."

Quickly, she drew a pistol from the desk. "Now, get out, Dilcher, before I send for the citizens' committee."

Snarling, he said, "You haven't heard the last of me, *Mrs. Whitley.*"

Alex entered the office as the trio walked away, and he said, "What did they want?"

Now that the crisis had passed, Unity's legs trembled, and she sat down weakly. "Money! I chased them away. Let's hope they stay chased."

"It's too bad we don't have a prison to jail some of these birds, but they are leaving town fast. Anyway, the citizens are converting the brig *Euphemia* into a jail, and it should be ready as soon as they fit it out with balls and chains and handcuffs."

When Matt returned from Sacramento City, Unity told him about the three Hounds who had confiscated the clothing, but she withheld any information about Dilcher. Even though her conscience warned that she should tell him everything, she was too much of a coward to jeopardize his good opinion of her. Especially now, when Matt was so interested in building their home, she didn't have the heart to disillusion him.

As they wound through the dusty streets in a rented carriage and started climbing the hill behind the city to the site Matt had chosen, he said, "We'll need a carriage of our own when the house is completed."

"Yes, I can see I'll be a long way from the office."

"Unity, don't you ever expect to stop working and just be my wife? I'd like that."

"I don't know what I'd do with the business, and I can't make any decision without consulting my sister. After all, she is part owner. If only we had the telegraph across the continent, I'd know what's going on back there. Now that Isaac is dead, I fear for the future of Spencer Shipping."

"I hadn't thought much about a family until Becky was here with David, but I'd like a son, Unity. I hope we won't have to wait much longer. I'm approaching middle age, and I don't want to be so old I won't enjoy my children."

Unity laid her hand on his arm. "I want a child as much

as you do, Matt, and perhaps we will have one soon after we marry, but the conception of children doesn't always take place when we expect it. Don't worry, if God gives us some children, I'll leave the business in Alex's hands."

They stood on a wide acreage atop a bluff facing San Francisco Bay. A strong breeze riffled their clothing as they examined the place where Matt wanted to build their home. "If the house overlooks the city, there will be plenty of room for a stable and other outbuildings. Do you like it, Unity?"

Beyond the bay, she glimpsed the ocean waves, but her attention was drawn to the cluttered city below them where tents, ramshackle buildings, and shacks mingled with a few pretentious brick edifices. Almost two hundred ships lay at anchor in the harbor, while others had been beached for businesses. She could see the huge brig in use as a prison, and she knew that other ships housed banks and at least one church.

With its hodgepodge of buildings and struggling humanity, San Francisco must be the ugliest city on earth, she thought. Yet as she stared at it, Unity sensed a surge of pride. She'd had the opportunity to share in the growth of this ungainly, struggling giant.

In a moment of joy she imagined raising a family here; she and Matt could grow old together in this spot. Unity threw her arms around him. "I'd love to have a home on this site. I think I could be very happy here for the rest of my life. I love you, Matt."

Suddenly the good feeling faded, and cold chills coursed through her body as she remembered Samuel Whitley and Micah Dilcher, two people who definitely stood between her and a happy future. Hiding her head on Matt's shoulder, Unity repeated, "I love you, Matt. Whatever you hear, whatever might happen in the future, don't forget, I love you."

They spent more than an hour at the site, deciding on the location of the outbuildings and the style of the house. "I'd like a house similar to our family home in Boston, if that suits you," Unity suggested.

"Whatever you want. I'm building this house for you. Draw up a plan and send it to the contractor. He's ready to start."

The new house developed quickly, and each time Matt was in San Francisco, he and Unity hurried to the building to check its progress. On one of their trips, as they ascended the hill and before they lost sight of the harbor, Matt said, "Looks like another ship is entering the Golden Gate. I believe it's a clipper."

"Oh, perhaps it's ours. If so, I hope the captain can keep his crew this time, I'd prefer not to have the ship laid up as long as it was the last voyage."

"If he does lose the crew, I think he'll find enough home-sick sailors to take the ship home. More and more people are realizing they can't make a fortune, and they've already spent the money they brought with them. Seldom do I leave Sacramento City that I don't bring back several men who can't pay their fare. All they want to do is to go home."

Due to the vast maze of ship's riggings, Unity couldn't pick out the clipper when they arrived back at the waterfront. If the vessel did belong to Spencer Shipping, perhaps she'd have a letter from Boston.

As they shared dinner Matt was as animated as Unity had ever seen him, and their evening promised to be one of celebration. They'd hardly settled in the living room, however, when a gentle tap sounded on the door. When she was alone, Unity dreaded the thought of a night caller, but perhaps this was Sid, who often came to share their company when Matt visited her.

When Matt opened the door, not Sid's, but a woman's voice asked, "Does Unity Spencer live here?"

For a moment, Unity couldn't place the voice, but when Matt wordlessly stood aside and motioned the woman into the room, Unity bounced out of her chair as if she'd been stung. There was no mistaking the stalwart figure of Deborah Jenkins. Startled, at first Unity didn't notice what the woman held in her arms.

"Levi?" she murmured, looking in stunned disbelief at the child, but there was no mistaking the Whitley features, especially the cleft chin so prominent in the boy's face.

Deborah stood the boy on his feet and said, "This is your mother, Levi. I've told you about her."

Unity, tears streaming down her face, sank to her knees and held out her hands to the son she hadn't seen for more than a year. Levi looked uncertainly at Deborah, and then hesitantly he wobbled across the floor.

Unity snatched him into her arms. Over his head, she intercepted Matt's disillusioned stare. She'd completely forgotten his presence. Only a moment did their glances hold before Matt bolted out the door.

Lifting the wriggling child to her lap, Unity sat on the davenport and motioned Deborah to a seat. Levi squirmed out of her grasp and ran to Deborah. Nestling the boy in her arms, Deborah said, "It will take him a while to get used to you, though I've been trying to prepare him for a new mother since we left Boston."

"Maybe you'd better tell me what brought all of this on. I can't comprehend it yet."

"Margaret remarried in January. When she learned she was with child, she didn't want Levi anymore. There has never been any affection between them, as you know. She's sent him back to you. It's just that simple. You know Margaret—no consideration for anyone except herself."

"I'm happy to have him; I've never gotten over the pain of leaving him, but I wish I'd had a little warning. I'm engaged and my betrothed didn't know that I had a child. This came as quite a shock to him."

"I could see that, Miss Unity, and I'm sorry, but I didn't know what else to do. I thought you'd want the boy."

"Oh, I do, but I'm sorry that Matt had to find it out in such a shocking manner."

Opening the reticule she carried, Deborah removed a letter, which she handed to Unity.

"Dear Unity," Margaret had written:

> As you will have learned by now from Deborah, I've remarried, and will soon be bearing a child of my own. All of these years, when I thought that I was infertile, the fault must have been Isaac's, because I became with child almost at once after I married my present husband, Jeremiah. With a child of our own, I don't think I should keep Levi to share in *my* children's inheritance.
>
> Speaking of inheritance, Jeremiah is operating Spencer Shipping here in Boston, and we've wondered if you'd be willing to exchange your share of the eastern branch of the company for our portion of what is in San Francisco. Jeremiah thinks that's a fair division. If you agree, sign the enclosed papers and return them to us. Please send your decision in the next mail.

Laying aside Margaret's letter, Unity asked, "What do you think of Margaret's husband?"

Deborah laughed. "He's a godsend for the business and for Miss Margaret. He knows how to keep her in line, and she's acting the way a Spencer ought to."

"Do you intend to stay here?"

"If you'll have me. I'd hate to leave the little tyke now; I've had the sole care of him for months."

"Then I know he's been in good hands, and of course I want you to stay. We'll be crowded at first, but Matt and I are building a new house, and once we marry we'll have plenty of room."

Unity watched Levi as he slept in Deborah's arms. She had her son now, but had she lost Matt? The look on his face when he'd stumbled from the room haunted her.

When the child ran to Unity and acknowledged her as his mother, anger had swelled up in Matt, wild rage that he'd experienced only twice before. The first time was when he realized that his mother would bear an illegitimate child and the other time when he learned that Becky and Maurie loved each other, and he'd thought that Becky had betrayed his trust.

He staggered from the deck of the houseboat and ran away from the harbor, trying to escape the obvious fact that Unity was the mother of that boy. Why hadn't she told him? He could have accepted the fact. After all, she'd been married, and it would have been normal for her to have a child. Then, dumbstruck, he teetered on the edge of the wharf. The fishy smell of the water filtered around him, but he was unaware of his surroundings, when the thought entered his mind, *Did the child belong to her husband?*

"God," he whispered, "I can't bear another shock like this. My mother was bad enough, but to find out that Unity's unchaste will be my undoing."

Hardly conscious of his actions, he moved forward and fell into the harbor. As the water closed over his head, Matt thought, *This could be the easy way out. If I drown, I won't have to face this unpleasantness.* But he bobbed to the surface and caught hold of a pier. Taking a deep breath, he struggled back on the dock.

Wandering aimlessly, Matt finally reached the *Allegheny* and climbed to the pilothouse. He didn't even change his clothes, but sat on a bench and lowered his head to his hands. Hearing a light step, he raised his face. Unity stood beside him, and in the light from the lantern hanging on the bow of the boat, he observed the guilty expression on her face.

He stood up and faced the harbor, not looking at her again while she was in the pilothouse.

"I'd like to ask for your forgiveness, Matt, but I suppose that's expecting too much."

The agony in her voice moved him, but he couldn't answer.

"I know it was unforgivable not to tell you, but in a way, I was under obligation to keep his birth a secret. My first husband's family are terrible people, and because I feared they'd take my son away from me, if they knew I had one, I let my childless sister persuade me to give her the child."

At least the child was legitimate.

"No one knew about the baby except the two of us and Deborah; she'd been our housekeeper for years. I've always been sorry that I agreed to my sister's terms, but I didn't know what else to do. I was trying to protect my son. I promised Margaret I'd never tell anyone that Levi wasn't hers."

So the Levi she'd called for in her sleep was a son.

It wasn't as bad as Matt had feared, yet he couldn't see why she hadn't trusted him with the information.

"Margaret has remarried and is expecting a child of her own, so she sent my boy to me. I wish you'd talk to me, Matt. Please say something. I'm suffering the same as you."

"I *can't* talk to you," he blurted out at last. "I'm not sure I ever want to see you again. I thought you were all that was perfect in a woman, and I can't bear to know that you've been engaged to me for months without telling me you had a child. I'm just glad we never married. Leave me alone."

She laid her hand on his arm. He tensed, but he didn't turn toward her. "Matt, remember what I told you earlier, 'No matter what happens, I want you to know I love you.' You're the most precious person in the world to me, more important even than my son. That's the reason I wanted you to think I was perfect."

She removed her hand, and for several more minutes Matt stood silently. When he turned at last, Unity had gone.

10

*T*he *Allegheny* was still moored at the wharf the next morning, when Unity looked out. She had tried to sleep on the sofa after she left Matt, but she couldn't remain immobile. She paced the floor the rest of the night, listening in vain for the sound of Matt's footsteps, hoping he'd come to say he'd forgiven her.

The fog lifted early, and soon Unity heard the blast of the *Allegheny*'s whistle. He was leaving without coming to her. Unity's sorrow was too great for tears as she reconciled herself to a life without Matt. After the love they'd shared, how could he walk out of her life?

Hearing soft steps in the bedroom, Unity pecked on the door, and Deborah opened it. "The little tyke is still sleeping," she whispered. Unity walked quietly into the room and gazed at Levi. Lying on his back, he breathed evenly, a soft smile on his face. *Son or husband?* It seemed she could have one or the other, but in spite of Matt's attitude, she couldn't be sorry that Levi was safe with her.

Then apprehension nearly suffocated Unity when she remembered that the continent no longer separated Levi from his father. His reddish hair was the only Spencer feature that the boy had inherited; otherwise he looked like the Whitleys, and if Samuel were ever to see Levi, he'd know the child belonged to him. And what if Matt discovered that Samuel was alive? Unity shook her head in disbelief that all of these things had happened. Was God punishing her for her sins?

Suddenly she remembered a Psalm she'd learned in her youth: "Who shall ascend into the hill of the Lord? or who shall stand in his holy place? He that hath clean hands, and a pure heart; who hath not lifted up his soul unto vanity, nor sworn deceitfully." Her pact with Margaret concerning Levi had been a mistake from the beginning. They'd deceived Isaac, and that had led to her deceiving Matt. Nothing had worked out as they'd thought it would. How much simpler it would have been to have kept Levi and depended upon God's guidance to prevent the Whitley's from claiming him!

Yet God still kept me in His love, Unity realized with wonder. *He brought Levi back to me, from a continent away. Though I'd nothing but hate for Samuel, He showed me the love of a godly man.* How glad she was that she knew Matt's love.

O Lord, she prayed, *can You make things right?* Into her mind flooded the story of Sarah and Abraham. The Bible told how they'd manipulated a child for their own purposes, yet God had forgiven them. *Will You forgive me, too?* Offering up her wrongs to God, Unity felt His forgiveness rush over her being.

She was right with God. Now could Matt forgive her?

As they ate the breakfast Jiang had prepared, Unity said to Deborah, "I must go to the office soon. With all of the clipper's produce to unload and tally, I'll be busy for a few days. Can you take care of yourself and the child, until we can make plans?"

"Yes, don't worry about me. I need some time to rest after that journey." She hesitated, then continued, "I did bring those papers you asked for—from the lawyer, I mean."

Her words brought Unity a sense of relief. If Matt did learn about Samuel, then she had proof that he was no longer her husband. But would Matt even care anymore?

Alex's joyous face contrasted with her own, when she entered the office.

"I've asked her, Unity. She's willing, and so are her parents."

Unity reached for his hand and forced a smile. At least someone could be happy, and she didn't want to spoil Alex's joy by revealing her own wretchedness. "Will you marry soon?"

"A Chinese marriage doesn't take long. Lin said I should buy two gold rings, and when Wang placed them in her earlobes, that would show her willingness to be my wife."

"Surely you'll want more of a ceremony than that!"

He laughed. "Yes. I've finally fitted out a boat for the Chinese church, and I thought we could have our wedding there in a few weeks. Several preachers have come to San Francisco, and I'll find one to perform the ceremony."

"I'm expecting you to take some time off. Go to the rancho for several days; Uncle John will want you to come."

The farther the *Allegheny* traveled away from San Francisco, the more Matt became convinced that he'd acted like a fool. Why did he find it so hard to be reasonable? He'd been unforgiving toward his mother and Becky and now with Unity. At least he could have listened to what she had to tell him. Why did he always hurt the ones he loved the most? Then he realized that was his trouble. He had deeply loved only three people, and he was vulnerable where they were concerned. The devil must ride on his back all the time. After the happiness he'd known with Unity, why had he muffed it?

Long before he reached Sacramento City, he'd made up his mind to ask Unity's forgiveness, and Matt chafed during the time it took to unload his cargo. He acknowledged his own morose mood, but somehow, when he finally pulled away from the dock, with a blast on the *Allegheny*'s whistle, the jollity of the Frisco-bound passengers grated on his nerves.

Although his rules prohibited drinking on board the packet, he felt convinced that three of the travelers had a bottle with them. "Who are those men?" Matt demanded when Sid joined him in the pilothouse.

"Who knows anybody's name now?" Sid responded with disgust. "A year ago, when this gold rush started, everyone was honest, but hundreds of rough characters have rolled in now. People use nicknames more than their real names. That guy with the twitching eye uses the name of Dilcher; the tall man with the cleft chin is called Big Sam; and the other one is Albany Pete. I've seen Pete before, and I'm sure he was one of the Hounds the citizens chased out of Frisco a few weeks ago. We'd all have been better off if they'd stayed in the gold fields."

"*Dilcher*? That name sounds familiar. I believe we saw him in Monterey. He was in the army then, so I suppose he's another soldier who's left his seven dollars a month to make a fortune in the creeks of California. A lot of thugs will be moving back before the wet weather starts. Keep your eye on them."

But after their first rollicking day, the three men settled

down and caused no trouble. Dilcher sauntered into the pilothouse several times and tried to engage Matt in conversation, but Matt's mind and heart were too heavy for talking. All he wanted was to reach San Francisco and make his peace with Unity.

By mid-afternoon on their third day out of Sacramento, Matt nosed the *Allegheny* into its accustomed place at the docks. Looking toward Unity's houseboat, he saw no sign of life, so he supposed she was still at the warehouse. When the engine ceased, Matt left the pilothouse to help Sid direct the crew as they unloaded. All the passengers had gone except Dilcher, who stood beside the rail, looking at Matt with a stupid grin on his face.

Dilcher lingered until the deck was cleared of boxes and the Chinese crew hurried off. He strolled over to where Matt waited impatiently near the gangplank.

"I wanted to talk to you alone, Mr. Miller—figured you might not want anyone to hear what I have to say to you. My luck was all bad up at the diggings, and I'm a poor man. I've noticed you've got a prosperous business here— a good boat and lots of revenue coming in."

"Get to the point, buddy. I have a good business because I work at it."

"I wonder how much you'd pay for some information I know about Unity Spencer or how much it would be worth to you for me not to tell anyone else?"

Ungovernable rage boiled up in Matt, and he thought his head would explode. Dilcher's face blurred before him, and he swung blindly, but the blow connected, for he heard the snap of the man's neck as he toppled off the gangplank. Matt quivered in every muscle, and he staggered when Sid rushed by him to pull the floundering Dilcher out of the water.

Dilcher lay on the dock, stunned. With Sid's urging, he

sat up and struggled to his feet. Blood gushed from his face, and it looked as if Dilcher's nose was broken.

"That's my answer, Dilcher. Don't come around me again."

Unity heard the *Allegheny*'s whistle when Matt entered the harbor. Only the strongest willpower kept her from leaving the office and rushing to him, but she wouldn't take the chance of being rejected again. When more than two hours passed and Matt hadn't shown up, she accepted the fact that he was through with her. She dreaded returning to the houseboat, knowing that he was in town and that she couldn't even talk to him.

Because Deborah would be waiting for her, Unity didn't delay any longer. With downcast eyes, she left the office and started down the steps from the warehouse. She became aware of someone standing in front of her, and when she looked up, Matt stood a few feet away. Their gazes held for a moment, until Matt opened his arms, and she ran to him.

"Oh, Matt," she breathed, "I've been miserable without you. Can you ever forgive me? I can explain everything."

"I should have let you talk, but I love you so much, Unity, that I couldn't accept that you'd been dishonest with me. I suppose I'm jealous."

"You're still first, Matt, don't you know that? Come, I want you to meet my son."

With a wry smile, Matt said, "I know I told you I wanted a son, but I didn't expect you to produce one before we even married."

"It's a long story, and I'll tell you all about it."

He hugged her to him, and with his arm still around her shoulders, they went toward the harbor.

They encountered Deborah and Levi in the living room.

Levi was playing on the floor with a toy dog that Unity had found in a shipment from Boston. When he saw Matt, the child scampered toward Deborah and hid behind her skirts. Hoping this wasn't a portent of the future relationship between the two, Unity picked up her child.

"See what a fine boy he is, Matt." Levi gave Matt a hasty glance from his blue eyes, and when Unity would have passed him to Matt, he hid his face on her shoulder.

"He's not used to men yet, Miss Unity. Give him time, and he'll come around."

Matt was introduced to Deborah, and they sat down, but their conversation was stilted. Finally, Unity said, "I haven't seen Matt for several days, so if you and Levi can manage tonight, I'll eat supper with him. We're right next door, if you need us, and of course, the Soongs are below deck."

"We'll be fine, Miss Unity. Go along."

Leaving the houseboat, Matt said apologetically, "I would have taken the boy, but I haven't held a child since Becky was a baby. I'm afraid I won't make a very good father."

Sid was ready to leave the *Allegheny* when they arrived, and he said, "Chang left some supper on the stove in the galley, boss. I'm going uptown."

"I don't want any unexpected company," Matt said, with a knowing look at Sid, "so I'm lifting the gangplank. Give me a whistle when you return."

Unity had intercepted the look between the two men, and she wondered what it meant.

"Maybe Chang didn't leave enough food for the two of us," she said as they entered the galley, but they found plenty to satisfy their hunger.

As soon as they had finished eating, Unity tried to get to the point.

"Matt, I'll try to explain," she started, but he interrupted, "Not now, Unity. I had more than one reason for lifting the gangplank, for I don't want any interruptions. I need to hear what you have to tell me, but more than that, I need the assurance that all is right between us."

He enveloped her in his arms with a grasp that left Unity breathless. Her hands moved around his neck, and Matt's lips sealed hers. Mutual forgiveness flowed from one to the other, and their deep love surfaced again.

Later Matt drew a deep sigh as he relaxed his embrace. "Now, I can listen to whatever you have to tell me."

Unity stirred listlessly. She hadn't had a good night's rest since Matt had rejected her, and now that all was well, she wanted to go to sleep, but she had promised Matt an explanation.

"I married Samuel Whitley in January of eighteen forty-seven," Unity began and poured out the circumstances of her marriage.

When he heard of her husband's life-style, Matt sat in shocked silence for a few seconds, then commented, "I don't blame any woman for not wanting to live with a man like that."

Encouraged, Unity continued, "I think I'd have jumped into the ocean, if Samuel hadn't disappeared on that fishing trip."

"Disappeared?"

Unity took a deep breath. "Samuel and two companions went out in a fishing yawl. A terrible storm raged up the coast that day. The boat and the bodies of the two other men washed ashore, but Samuel wasn't found.

"By then I'd found that I was expecting a child, and I determined that no child of mine would ever be raised in that Whitley household. I ran away one night and went back to my childhood home." After recounting the bargain she'd made with Margaret, she explained, "To protect Levi as much as possible from the Whitleys, I arranged for a divorce from Samuel. The courts aren't very sympathetic to that type of thing, and while I didn't think Samuel could possibly be living, I wanted to be sure that I was free from him."

"And Isaac didn't know the truth either?"

"No. Levi was five months old when he returned from a sea voyage. Margaret was jealous of Levi and me, and the situation became intolerable. If Isaac hadn't gotten ill, I'd have brought Levi with me when I came to California, but I feared if he knew that we'd deceived him, it would kill Isaac. For everybody's good, I thought it was better to leave."

"But why didn't you tell me? I can understand your reason for doing this, but didn't you trust me enough to confide in me?"

"It wasn't that. Somehow I just couldn't bring myself to destroy your faith in me. I feared that might be the case if you knew I'd abandoned my child."

"But why is he here now?"

"Margaret remarried, found herself with child almost immediately, and she no longer wanted Levi. He had never made up to Margaret anyway. So Deborah brought him to me."

"I'll help you care for him, Unity, so don't worry about the Whitleys any longer."

"Margaret wrote, wanting to divide the company with me. I'd take control of the business in San Francisco and the ships here and leave her control of the assets in the East. Does that meet with your approval?"

"Yes. If you're the sole owner, perhaps you can make Alex the manager and settle down and be my wife."

Before Unity could finish her story, several sharp whistles sounded, and Matt said, "That's Sid. I'll let him aboard, take you home, and bed down for the night. I haven't slept for over a week."

By the time Matt returned, where, an hour ago, she had been ready for sleep, now Unity was tense and wide awake. When could she share with Matt that she knew Samuel was still alive and in California? She'd have no peace until she held no secrets from Matt. *But after all, we are divorced,* she comforted herself. *Samuel has no legal claim. Now that Matt knows the truth about my husband, he could not believe our divorce is wrong.* But would Matt marry a divorced woman?

Having made his reconciliation with Unity, Matt's mind was alerted to other matters. What had Dilcher wanted to tell him about her? Could the man have known about her marriage and the birth of her child? Or was there something else? Matt's peace of mind fled, and that night he slept little.

The next day the couple attended the simple wedding ceremony uniting Alex and Wang. As she looked around the small room that Alex had reclaimed for church services, Unity realized that the months they'd spent introducing the Chinese to Western culture had been worthwhile. Only a few of the Asians had been converted to Christianity, but it was a beginning.

Telling himself he had exaggerated fears about Unity, Matt focused all his thoughts on the new house, pleased to be building the kind of house Unity wanted.

Once she had asked, "Do you think we should build a Spanish-type house? A New England house may look out of place here."

But when they consulted her uncle, who had come to San Francisco on business, John advised, "Build what you like. Most of the people who are building now in San Francisco wouldn't know how to construct an adobe house."

John had enthusiastically shared his ideas for the construction, still remembering his days in Boston. Somewhat surprised at his excitement, Unity had asked, "Uncle John, are you ever homesick for the East?"

"Oh, sometimes, I suppose, but even if I were to return, after eleven years, the changes would be so great I wouldn't feel comfortable. Besides, it's a great experience to be on the ground floor when a new state develops. Do you know they're already talking about California statehood?"

"No, I hadn't heard so," Matt had admitted. "Are there enough people here to form a state?"

"We have near one hundred thousand people in the territory, I've heard, and the population only had to reach sixty thousand to draw up a constitution. By this time next year, we'll be living in a state, rather than a territory." With a smile at Unity, he had added, "So I will be living at 'home.' "

They had agreed upon a sprawling three-storied, twelve-room house, constructed of lumber with a shingled roof. The contractor had recently arrived from New York, and he was familiar with New England houses.

"The downstairs should have a kitchen and dining area, as well as a family living room, and a large room for entertaining. We'll have five bedrooms on the second floor, and a nursery, as well as two rooms on the third floor for domestic help."

"Whatever you want, Unity. I've lived on boats most of my life, remember, so I don't know much about houses."

The contractor promised that they'd be in their new house by Christmas. With that thought in mind, Unity considered what she would do for furniture. Mail service provided fairly rapid communication with the East now, on United States government ships that plied the Atlantic and Pacific, with a land crossing at Panama.

If she made out an order for furniture and sent it by the next steamer, it would still take several months for the items to travel to her, which would mean delaying a move into the new house. As she pondered over what items to order and how she could adequately make her wants known to the furniture maker in Boston, Unity heard the door open and someone enter the office.

She made one last notation on the order page and looked up at her visitor. Her heart lurched, and she felt as a drowning victim must feel when he gives up the struggle and succumbs to the pull of the water. She had worse problems than furnishing a new house.

Samuel Whitley stood before her, and the self-satisfied look on his face reminded Unity of a cat that had finally cornered its prey. She wondered if she looked as desperate as she felt.

11

*U*nity's throat tightened until she thought she would choke, and she half rose from her chair. Two thoughts flitted through her mind, *I'm glad Matt is on his way to Sacramento City,* and, *I wish Levi were back in Boston.*

She couldn't speak, and Samuel seemed to be enjoying this moment of surprise, smiling at her, toying with her emotions.

"How are you today, Mrs. Unity Spencer Whitley?"

Determined that this man wouldn't cow her, she said tersely, "I was fine until you came, and I'd appreciate having you leave immediately."

"Is that any way to talk to a husband you haven't seen for over two years?" Samuel said as he sprawled on the bench in front of her desk.

"You don't happen to be my husband anymore!"

He lifted his eyebrows. "I know you're engaged to another man, but it doesn't change the fact that you're my wife. How low the righteous Spencers have fallen!"

"Since your body wasn't recovered from that shipwreck, before I left Boston I obtained a divorce from you. I didn't suppose, then, that I'd want to marry again; life with you had made me immune. But I didn't want your questionable end to control the rest of my life."

Gratified that her voice didn't mirror the trauma she felt, Unity rose on legs that wobbled slightly and went to the safe in the corner. Whirling the combination with unsteady fingers, she lifted out a legal document, which she handed to Samuel. He glanced through it, then contemptuously threw the paper in front of her. She returned the document to the safe, knowing that Samuel wouldn't hesitate to destroy the proof that she no longer belonged to him.

Sneering, he said, "Do you think I care whether or not you're my wife? A colder, more boring woman I've never touched. I wouldn't have married you in the first place if your old man hadn't tempted me with the Spencer fortune."

"Then you and my father were well matched. Don't flatter yourself that he thought you were heaven's gift of a husband—he wanted the Whitley shipping. Why I had to become a pawn in your deals, I don't know. It serves both of you right that no money exchanged hands."

Samuel stared at her appraisingly for several minutes. "I'm beginning to believe that my appearance here this morning didn't take you by surprise."

"I saw you several months ago in Sacramento City, but I didn't know you were in this town. Did you strike it rich?"

"No, I didn't, and I want to go home. There's no need for me to be grubbing in the dirt, looking for gold, when there's plenty waiting for me in Rhode Island."

"Why did you disappear without a word? Though you

didn't care what I thought, at least you should have considered your parents. They believed you were dead."

"I might as well have been," Samuel replied bitterly. "When our fishing boat was torn apart in that storm, I hung on to the wreckage and was picked up by a Spanish ship. I was a captive on that stinking boat for months, and I couldn't escape. They sailed to Europe, then to the Sandwich Islands, and didn't put into an American port until a few months ago, when they landed at Monterey. I saw my chance and jumped ship. I sent my parents a letter then, the first opportunity I'd had to do it."

Although Unity had thought she could never feel pity for Samuel, she did at that moment. How it must have wounded his pride to be reduced to a shanghaied seaman and to be cut off from his family. In spite of his evil ways, Samuel was fond of his parents.

"Then I guess the Spanish repaid the Whitleys for all of their ships your father plundered."

Unity thought she'd pushed Samuel too far, and he lifted his hand to strike her. He controlled his anger and said, "I'm ready to go home, and I need some money."

"From me, you mean?"

"That's right. I don't want to wait for money to come from my parents."

"There's a Spencer ship leaving for Boston tomorrow. I can guarantee you free passage on that, and I will give you some spending money, but not a great deal. I'm short of money, too."

Samuel surveyed her with a shrewd look. "You seem anxious to get rid of me. Does Miller know you've been married before?"

"Certainly."

She didn't like his calculating look. "I mean, does he know I'm still alive?"

She stared at him, refusing to answer.

"Ah-ha! So he doesn't. Well, my dear Unity, it may take more than you anticipate to ship me eastward."

"You'll need very little except your boat passage. I've told you I don't have much money. We're building a house, and that's taken all of our funds right now. So don't try to rob me."

A step at the door alerted Unity, and as she looked, expecting to see Lin, deep anguish surged through her body. She dropped into the chair. Deborah stood in the doorway, with Levi in her arms.

"Mama," Levi shouted and waved his hand. Deborah placed the child on the floor, and he ran toward Unity. The horror on her face must have alerted Deborah, and for the first time she looked at Unity's visitor. Recognition came slowly, but when it did, Deborah collapsed on the floor.

Samuel jumped to his feet and started to the aid of the woman before he had his first look at Levi, who had clambered to his mother's lap. Unity wanted to wrap the child in her arms to shield him from Samuel's scrutiny, but it was too late. Even without her frenzied expression and Deborah's collapse, her former husband had already recognized the Whitley features on the face of his son.

"So this is the reason you were so eager to have me leave California!"

Levi regarded the stranger with piercing blue eyes exactly like Samuel's. He lifted his hand and waved.

Samuel moved closer, touched the reddish curls, and laid his forefinger along the cleft in the child's chin.

"Hello, little man! What's your name?"

"Levi."

"How old are you?"

Levi looked at his mother, who remained silent.

"How old is he?" Samuel demanded.

Unity stared at him.

"So you'd deny me my son, would you? Knowing how much this child would mean to my parents, you deliberately brought him out here!" He turned on his heel and paused at the door. "Don't bother booking passage for me on the Spencer ship. I'm going home, all right, but when I go, I'm taking my son with me."

Unity clutched Levi so tightly that the boy wriggled and started to cry. Noticing that Deborah was stirring, she placed Levi on the floor and went to assist the older woman to a sitting position. Deborah looked around the room with glazed eyes, and noting that Samuel was gone, she moistened her lips with her tongue and mumbled, "I'm sorry, Miss Unity. It was such a pretty day, and the little tyke had been asking for you. Where did *he* come from?"

"I can explain later. Right now we must act quickly to prevent him from taking Levi. Go to the houseboat, pack some clothes for yourself and Levi, and prepare to leave."

She helped Deborah to her feet and whirled when Lin entered the office.

"Go to the hotel and see if Uncle John has left for the rancho yet. If he hasn't, tell him I want to see him immediately."

As soon as the others left the office, Unity snatched up a shawl and ran toward the harbor. A Spencer ship lay at anchor, out in the bay, and she successfully signaled the captain to send a skiff for her.

"How soon can you leave here?" she asked when they were closeted in the captain's stateroom. Captain Adams was one of the oldest employees of Spencer Shipping, and she trusted his discretion completely.

"In a few hours, if necessary. Our cargo is loaded, but we'll have to round up the crew."

"Do that," she commanded, explaining her predicament and what she wanted him to do.

Stopping at the houseboat on her return, she found Deborah ready to leave. "Have Lin carry your things to the Spencer ship as soon as possible. I'll not feel safe until I know Levi's on that ship, leaving the bay."

To her relief, John Spencer waited in the office. She paused a moment to catch her breath.

"What's the matter, Unity? You look as if you've been sick for a month."

"My former husband, Samuel Whitley, came into the office this morning. While he was here, Deborah brought Levi in, and since the child looks so much like the Whitleys, it didn't take Samuel long to tumble to the fact that the child was his. He told me he was taking my boy away from me, and I *will not* let the Whitleys have that child."

"I thought he was dead." Surprise clung to her uncle's features.

"I thought that, too, when I came west, but he isn't." Out swept the whole story she had tried so hard to keep from Matt. "I hate to be drawn into more deception, but I must hide Levi from him. God gave that child to me. Can I do anything but protect him from harm?"

Her uncle didn't hesitate a moment.

"How can I help?"

"I've already made arrangements. There's a Spencer ship leaving here today, and Deborah and Levi will be on board. I'm hoping Samuel will believe they're on their way to Boston. Actually, I've asked the captain to go ashore below Monterey where our ships stop to pick up hides from the Alvarado rancho. Captain Adams has worked for us in the California trade for years, and he knows where the landing is. Will you give Deborah and Levi sanctuary until Samuel leaves California?"

John rose purposefully and clamped his wide-brimmed hat on his head. "I'll leave within the hour. Don't worry about the child; he'll be safe with me."

Returning to the houseboat, Unity met Lin, who came from the wharf. "Did they go aboard the ship?"

"Yes, missy. Safe on board."

"Do me a favor, please. Go back and watch until that ship leaves the harbor, and be sure nobody removes Levi."

Taking her field glasses, Unity hired a carriage to take her to the building site. From a vantage point, she picked out the Spencer ship and watched as it lifted anchor and eased out of the Golden Gate. For a moment, Levi was safe, but deep inside, she knew that the boy would never be safe as long as Samuel lived. Even if he didn't want his son, Samuel would take him to punish her, and Samuel's father would do anything in his power, legally or not, to gain guardianship of his grandson.

When Lin assured her that no man resembling Samuel had boarded the Spencer ship, Unity breathed easier. For the moment, at least, Levi was out of Samuel's clutches, but she faced another problem. As soon as Matt returned, she *had* to tell him that Samuel was alive. The deceit over Levi had been bad enough. He'd forgiven her for that and had grown fond of the boy. If only she'd had time to tell Matt of her husband before he'd sailed. But Sid had interrupted them, and Alex's wedding had not seemed the time to unload such a secret on him.

Having slept little, Unity was in no condition for more friction the next morning when Samuel came to the office accompanied by two men. Dilcher was one of them, and his presence gave Unity a start.

Samuel introduced the other man as a lawyer, and he probably was, for lawyers were numerous in Frisco right now. "I've taken legal steps to gain custody of my son."

"You have no proof that he's your son, Samuel."

"No proof," he shouted, "when his face mirrors mine."

The lawyer handed her a paper that looked legal enough, but Unity had enough intelligence to know that it probably wasn't. Obviously this was a plot to scare her into giving up the boy.

She took the paper, however, stating, "When do you want him?"

Surprised, Samuel stared at her silently, as if he hadn't considered what he would do with a two-year-old boy.

"Tomorrow."

"I'll give it some thought" was all she said.

After the lawyer left, Dilcher cleared his throat. "Big Sam, if you really want any proof that the child is yours, I might be able to supply it, for a price."

Samuel turned angrily toward him. "Dilcher, you've been following me around for weeks, hinting at the information you have. I don't need any proof that the boy is mine; he looks like me, and we were married at the time the child was conceived. Besides, as much as I dislike Unity, I'd never believe that she would bear an illegitimate child." He grabbed Dilcher by the shoulders and shook him like a rag. "I'm tired of your hints; tell me what you know, and don't expect any money out of it either."

Dilcher tightened his lips, but when Samuel continued shaking, he said, "Enough. Leave me alone."

Samuel threw the man from him, and Dilcher, straightening his clothes, started to leave the room. Samuel barred his way and grabbed the man by the throat. "Not until you tell me what you know."

Fright filled Dilcher's face. He couldn't wait to speak.

"I'm a doctor, and I was called in to assist when she had a child. That was in September or October, two years ago, right before I came to California. She hadn't even heard of Miller then."

Samuel pushed Dilcher to one side, and he slid down the wall to the floor. "You think I'd pay money for that? Any fool could have figured out that information." To Unity, he said, "I'll see you tomorrow."

Dilcher stared after him with raw hatred in his eyes. He included Unity in his venomous look before he left the office. Suddenly Unity wished she'd gone with Deborah and Levi, for she feared Dilcher. He had a warped mind, and it was hard to tell what he would do. She longed for Matt's presence, but still she didn't want him returning until Samuel had gone. If her plans went well, her former husband would soon be on his way to Boston.

By ten o'clock the next morning Samuel returned to the office. "Where's the boy?"

"Two days ago Deborah and Levi boarded a Boston-bound ship. By this time, they're safely out of your hands."

"You mean you dared to double-cross me?"

"You'll never take that child."

"You're as devious as your old man," Samuel snarled, "and probably as big a liar. I can soon find out if you're telling the truth. I don't know why you think that will help any. It will take me a little longer, but the courts in Boston will award me custody easily enough, when they learn that you're out of the States, and carrying on with another man."

He started around the desk toward her, and his sensuous laugh reminded her of all the depravity she had suffered at this man's hands. Her skin crawled with gooseflesh as she felt his huge body crowding her.

She backed out of his reach. "Don't ever touch me again, Samuel."

The door from the warehouse opened, and from the corner of her eye, Unity saw Lin and Alex standing behind her, guns drawn and aimed at Samuel.

He stopped his advances, and with a short laugh, admitted defeat. "You haven't heard the last of me," he threatened as he left the building.

The *Allegheny* was one day from San Francisco, and after they tied up for the night, Sid approached Matt in the pilothouse. He discussed details of tomorrow's landing, but when he lingered, Matt figured that his friend had something else on his mind.

"Boss, I've been wondering about that time you threw Dilcher in the harbor. Why'd you do that?"

"He made me mad."

"I sorta guessed that," Sid said wryly. "Let me put it another way. Has he suggested that he knew something about Miss Unity that he'd like to tell?"

"Yes, but I refused to listen to him."

"He approached me, too, when we were in Frisco the last time. I wrung the truth out him, and he told me some things I think you need to know."

Matt whirled on him angrily. "Why'd you do that?"

"Because I knew he would eventually sell his information to the highest bidder. I've grown fond of Miss Unity, and I don't want that scoundrel to cause her any trouble."

"I'm pretty fond of her myself; that's the reason I didn't want to hear him slander her."

"You told me once that Miss Unity had been married. Do you know that her husband is still living and is here in California?"

Matt whirled on Sid, who backed hastily out of his way. "She's a widow."

Sid shook his head stubbornly. "She may *think* she's a

widow, but Dilcher says her husband is alive, and I believe the man's telling the truth. Remember the time we brought Dilcher and his two buddies back from Sacramento City?"

Matt turned his back on Sid, but he nodded his head.

"The huge guy, the one they called Big Sam, is Samuel Whitley, Miss Unity's husband."

Slowly Matt had to accept the truth, and he said haltingly, "The man was lost at sea, and his body was never recovered, so this could be true, I suppose."

"I'm sorry I had to be the one to tell you, boss, but you had to know."

After Sid left the pilothouse, Matt dropped his head in his hands. Did Unity know? The thought haunted Matt. Had she known and not told him? Though she had divorce papers, it didn't alter the fact that she had living husband. The thought of his mother's moral lapse entered his mind, and he cringed. Were all women alike?

And that man was Levi's father! The reflection brought Matt to his feet, for he had started to think of Levi as his own son.

The *Allegheny* arrived at San Francisco in early afternoon. Normally Matt rushed to the Spencer warehouse as soon as he cleared the boat, but today he waited on the deck until he saw Unity coming home. In spite of what stood between them now, the sight of her caused his heart to miss a beat. He loved this woman, and without her, nothing much mattered. Would it be wiser to ignore Sid's information and go on as before? After all, she had no legal ties to this man. But Matt had never been a prudent man, and he threw caution to the winds.

Leaving the *Allegheny*, he met Unity in front of her houseboat. With a smile of welcome, she rushed to him.

When his arms didn't open to receive her, she stopped, a puzzled look on her face.

"Unity, do you know that Samuel Whitley is living and is here in California?"

Her face blanched, and she swayed on her feet, but he made no move to catch her. With blurred eyes, she admitted, "Yes. He came to the office a few days after you left."

"Is that the first time you'd known he was still alive?"

"He said that after the shipwreck we thought had taken his life, he'd been picked up by a Spanish boat and was forced into service on it. A few months ago, when the ship docked at an American port, he escaped."

"How long have you known he was in California?"

"It doesn't make any difference with us, Matt. I've told you, I never loved the man, and I have a divorce from him."

"How long have you known he was still living?"

She hesitated for a moment, but finally looking him in the eyes, she said bravely, "I saw him when we were in Sacramento City."

Without a word, Matt turned his back on her, boarded the *Allegheny*, and lifted the gangplank.

12

*A*fter he had learned she'd known about Samuel's reappearance, Matt didn't come near Unity. The suffering over his rejection was worse than the traumatic days she'd spent in the Whitley household and the time when she came to California, leaving Levi behind.

Yet I've only myself to blame, Unity decided. *Somehow I could have found a way to tell him before he found out for himself.*

She didn't suppose Matt knew Levi wasn't in San Francisco anymore, for with Samuel's reappearance, Matt wouldn't consider himself the boy's father. He'd probably lost interest in him. Deprived of both Matt and her son, Unity moped listlessly about the office.

The days were a fearful time, also, for Samuel Whitley shadowed her. He apparently hadn't believed that she'd sent the child to Boston, or perhaps he hadn't been able to get passage to the East, but he remained in town. Every place she went, he was there until she wondered if he ever slept.

Most of the day he sat near the Spencer office. When she went to bed at night, he was parked outside her house-boat, and he was still keeping vigil when she awakened in the morning. He didn't try to talk to her, he was just there, watching. She wondered if Matt had noticed Samuel's presence, but Matt seemed oblivious to anything concerning her. Sadly she wrote her uncle and canceled wedding plans.

One Sunday in early winter, after she and Alex had conducted services for the Chinese, she decided to go to the house site, and she asked Alex to order a carriage and ride along with her. She had taken on the responsibility for the property. The contractor was keeping to his schedule, and Unity had tried to direct the man's activities. Matt hadn't gone about the new house at all, though he seemed to have no objections to what she did. Unity had lost interest in the construction, but she had to have some place to live, especially if she could get rid of Samuel and bring Deborah and Levi back.

It had rained for a week, but today the clouds had rolled back to display a vivid blue sky, and Unity looked forward to being out of town. Actually, San Francisco was no longer a town—it had turned into a city. Asking Alex to stop the carriage on a vantage point not far from her new house, Unity viewed the place that had been her home for over a year.

The fleet of deserted ships in the bay numbered more than three hundred, and others were added daily. She looked at a forest of masts and spars with tangled lines and rigging. Many of the ships had almost sunk out of sight, because of leaky hulls, and others listed and swayed into their neighbors.

Quite a few of the deserted vessels had been beached by inventive men, who had converted them into stores and warehouses. These refurbished ships, intermingled with conventional buildings, spread out over the bay on wooden stilts. Streets were built of wooden planks, an improvement over the muddy thoroughfares they'd traversed last winter.

The city was not only ugly, it was lawless. After the rounding up of the Hounds earlier in the summer, groups of citizens had banded together to give the city some semblance of order, but the lawless element increased faster than the good citizens. Men arrived from countries all over the world, and the streets were crowded with gamblers, saloon keepers, thieves, murderers, and confidence men, as well as the responsible citizens who merely wanted to earn an honest living.

Unity forsook her reverie when she heard a carriage approaching. Samuel Whitley! Couldn't she escape him for a minute? Of course, when she left town, he thought she might be going to Levi's hiding place. Though she longed to see the boy, she knew she didn't dare visit or even send a message. She had received a communication from her uncle, stating, "The shipment has arrived in good order." She prayed that Samuel wouldn't think about John's rancho.

A quick survey of the house told her it would be ready for occupancy in a few weeks. Should she go ahead and move in? Obviously, Matt didn't intend to share it with her. Conscious of Samuel's waiting presence, she didn't tarry long, and while Alex drove back to town, they discussed having Christmas festivities for the Chinese church. Although Unity wasn't in a mood for celebrating, she knew their friends would be disappointed if they had no program.

The next morning, when Unity left the houseboat for the office, Samuel sat on the barrel where he often perched. Usually she passed by without a word, but finally her blood boiled, and she stopped.

"What do you hope to gain by shadowing me like this?"

"A son."

"I told you that Deborah and Levi left here the day you came to the Spencer office and threatened to take him. Do you think I could possibly have kept that child hidden for so long?"

"I'm beginning to think you did send him back to Boston, and I'm heading that way as soon as I can find a boat going to the East Coast. When I do, I'll take that loan you offered me."

"Anything to see the last of you. I'm warning you, Samuel, I'm weary of being followed, and I intend to get rid of you one way or another."

Then Unity noticed that two men who served on a citizens' committee to patrol the town stood nearby listening to their conversation. She flushed, and her pulse accelerated when she realized they'd heard her threaten Samuel.

Had her threat actually scared Samuel away? She couldn't imagine that her words could have intimidated him, but when she looked out of the window, the next morning, he wasn't watching from his usual spot. Before she finished her breakfast, someone pounded on the door. Unity waited breathlessly, hoping that it was Matt, for his boat should be back from Sacramento by now.

Jiang came in. "Two men to see you, missy."

The men stood on the walkway, and one motioned toward the gangplank. "What do you know about that?" he said, and following his pointing hand with her eyes, Unity knew why Samuel hadn't been watching her this morning. Sprawled on his back on the plank leading from her house to the boardwalk, her former husband stared upward with eyes that would never see again. His chest was smeared with blood.

"I don't know anything about it," she said, though her heart lurched with fear when she recognized her interrogator as one of the men who'd heard her threaten Samuel yesterday.

"Sure he didn't try to force himself in on you last night, and you shot him?"

"No!"

A crowd had gathered. Unity recognized Dilcher among them. He moved closer to the man who questioned Unity and said, "Mr. Whitley was a friend of mine, and he told me last night that this woman had threatened him. She wouldn't let him have his son. That's all he wanted from her."

Angry voices stirred among the watchers.

"Time people quit picking on the poor miners."

"She's a rich woman; they tell me she runs a bawdy house right here on this boat."

"Time to clean up this city."

"She has time for them yellow devils and then guns down a white man."

Unity couldn't believe that these miners would actually do her any harm, for in San Francisco, decent women were treated with respect. When one of the men took her arm and started to lead her away, she pulled back in protest.

"I tell you, I didn't shoot this man."

"Come along, ma'am. For your own protection, you'd better go with us."

Listening to the angry murmur of the crowd, she knew he was right. She'd made her friends among the Chinese, but they certainly didn't have any influence to help her. Eventually she could send word to John, and he'd come to her aid, but what would happen to her in the meantime? She knew many of the newcomers to the city resented the merchants, whom they accused of charging exorbitant prices for their goods. Spencer Shipping had come in for its share of censure. Even in the midst of her danger, as she walked by Samuel's lifeless body, Unity felt nothing but relief that this man was no longer a threat to Levi or to her.

A beached boat was used for an improvised courtroom, and whenever the occasion warranted, a jury of citizens were called to decide upon problems. Followed by a group of the mumbling miners, Unity was led into the structure.

"What's your name?" asked a man sitting behind the desk.

"Unity Spencer."

He looked at the two men who accompanied her, and they explained what had happened.

"Miss Spencer, as scarce as women are around here, I don't think we have a jury in town who'd convict a beautiful woman like yourself, but we'll have to hold you for a while," the clerk said.

"Hold me? Where?"

He motioned toward the harbor, where the prison ship, *Euphemia*, tugged slightly at its moorings. Stories she'd heard of the horrible conditions there made her skin crawl, and Unity, free for the moment, ran toward the door, but one of the men caught her by the wrist and pulled her to a sudden halt.

"Hold on, here. We're trying to clean up this town, and white woman or not, if you killed a man, you'll have to pay for it."

Holding tightly to her arm, the man steered her toward the dock. He forced her to enter a rowboat at the foot of a short flight of steps. "You're used to living on a boat, so it won't hurt you none to sleep here tonight. 'Course the rats may be a little more friendly in our facility." He laughed loudly at his poor effort at a joke.

On the *Euphemia*, Unity was led to a small cabin, which she suspected might belong to the jailer, but she felt relief that she wouldn't have to be below deck, in an open cell, with hardened criminals. Considering the riffraff walking the streets of San Francisco, she couldn't imagine how terrible the prisoners must be.

Matt had been in the city for several hours before he heard about Unity's arrest. Obliquely, he had watched the houseboat, and it seemed odd not to see any sign of life. For weeks, when he was tied up at the wharf, he'd looked for Levi, but today the boat had a deserted air.

Already sorry for his behavior toward Unity, he was ready to make amends. Even if he didn't feel free to be her husband under the circumstances, they could at least be friends. He'd hoped Unity would take the first step in effecting a reconciliation, but she hadn't come near the *Allegheny*. To be honest, he couldn't blame her, for he considered himself a despicable character.

Running steps approached the pilothouse, and he turned and looked into Sid's anxious eyes.

"What is it?" he demanded, while Sid gasped to catch his breath.

"Samuel Whitley was found dead on the gangway of Miss Unity's houseboat. They've arrested her for his murder. He'd been shot."

"Where is she?"

"She's being held on the *Euphemia*."

"That rat's nest!" Matt paced the floor, not knowing what to do. "Tell me everything you know."

"It seems that Miss Unity sent Levi away because Whitley intended to take him. That man's been following her for a month. I guess she got tired of it, and she was heard threatening him. When he was found dead near her boat, she was accused of his murder, although she says she's innocent."

Matt kicked the side of the pilothouse. "Sid, why don't you knock me on the head and throw me overboard?"

With an attempt at a smile, Sid said, "There have been times when that would have been a pleasure, but you can save me the trouble by jumping."

"*I'm* the one who deserves to be shot, going off in a pout and leaving Unity to face all this alone. I'd seen Whitley watching her boat, but for all I knew, they might have been making up their differences. It was jealousy, Sid. I tell you I should be shot."

"Shooting *you* won't help her. She's going to need all her friends. We have to find out who did shoot Whitley and make him confess. Without any law in this city, there won't be anyone else to do the investigation."

"Then you don't think she shot him?"

Sid looked at him in amazement. "Of course not, although she may have had reason to."

"You scout around the town, and I'll try to arrange for her release from that prison ship. Get hold of Dilcher; he might have some information to sell. If he does, buy it."

But no amount of argument on Matt's part would convince Unity's jailers to release her before the trial.

"Then I want to see her," Matt insisted. "I'm her betrothed."

The man looked up in surprise. "I thought she was in here for shooting her husband."

His words irritated Matt, but he knew he couldn't antagonize the man. "She was divorced from Whitley," he insisted.

"I suppose you can see her. Come along." Calling to a sentry on the bow of the ship, he said, "Send a boat over for this man. He wants to see the woman; give him a half hour."

After he suffered the indignity of being frisked by the jailer, Matt walked down the five steps to the water level and waited for the boatman. He stepped into the small boat, and the man silently rowed toward the *Euphemia*. Matt caught the swinging rope ladder and climbed to the deck. The sentry motioned Matt toward a small cabin at the rear of the ship. He knocked on the door, unlocked it, and allowed Matt to step inside.

The apprehension in Unity's eyes changed to joy when she saw her visitor. She ran to Matt, and he pulled her trembling body into a tight embrace, running his hands over her shoulders to reassure himself that he held her at last.

"Oh, Matt," she whispered, "I was feeling so alone."

"You're never going to be alone again. I've been a fool, but I'm cured. Will you forgive me once more?"

"I'm the one who should ask forgiveness. I should have told you about seeing Samuel in Sacramento City, but I didn't want to lose you. By the time I had the courage, things just got in the way. Will you believe me when I say that there is absolutely no other secret in my past that you don't know about?"

After he kissed her long and hard, Matt sat on the cot and drew her down beside him.

"The main thing now is to secure your release, and we'll have to plan fast. I have only a half hour. What happened anyway?"

Unity couldn't hold back any longer. How blessed to be able to right the wrongs that had troubled her for so long! The words tumbled out of her mouth until she had to gasp for breath. She ended, "I told Samuel that I'd put Levi on a Boston-bound boat, which was true, but he was still skeptical. He followed me everywhere, supposing that I'd lead him to Levi. I grew weary of his presence, and threatened him. The next morning he was found dead on my gangplank, and I was the logical suspect."

"Why? He must have made other enemies."

She nodded. "Samuel was the type to make enemies, but how will we find out who did this?"

"Sid is searching around now. He'll probably learn something. I hate to leave you here, but what else can I do? It won't be long. They'll have your trial tomorrow, the jailer said."

He kissed her again, and she whispered, "I didn't kill him, Matt, despite the pain he caused me. But we could never have been happy with the shadow of Samuel Whitley between us. It's difficult to forgive my father for marrying me to the man in the first place, but I'm learning some big lessons in forgiveness. I can see why Samuel wanted his son, who's the only direct heir to the Whitley fortune, but I couldn't send a child into that corrupt household."

"It will soon be behind us, so look up. Pray, Unity. My rebellious heart has prevented me from praying for weeks, but God can bring victory out of this."

That night Matt not only prayed, but he sat with the Bible in his hand for a long time, meditating upon Paul's words, "Husbands, love your wives, even as Christ also loved the church, and gave himself for it. . . . He that loveth his wife loveth himself." Could he marry Unity and love her that deeply?

Matt Miller had loved himself, but he had only judged Unity. To love his wife as Christ loved the church, he would have to be compassionate and forgiving. Unity's marriage and the subsequent birth of Levi had not been her own doing; she had bowed to her father's will. Matt recognized that even in withholding information from him she had been trying to protect her son.

I've spent most of my life being suspicious and unforgiving. It has to stop, Matt admitted to himself. *But, God, I'll need help. You've blessed me with everything a man could want—a good woman, a satisfying job, and riches. I'm tired of the old Matt Miller and his faults. God, make me a new man, one who's molded in Your image.*

Unity's trial was set for the day before Christmas, and as she waited in the small cell, she remembered a year ago. That was the day they'd had the program for the Chinese, the day she'd agreed to marry Matt. What a year it had been!

The grate of a key in the lock of her cell interrupted her reverie. The guard helped her down the rope ladder and into the boat. Matt waited for her when she arrived at the dock, and he took her hand as she climbed the steps. Quietly, she asked, "Have you learned anything?"

"No," he said cheerfully. "We'll have to rely on the common sense of the jury." But Unity could sense his concern.

A group of twelve men sat to one side of the small room, which seemed overcrowded with spectators. Even in boisterous, rowdy San Francisco, an American woman being tried for murder would draw a large crowd, especially when so many miners were idle during the rainy season.

After the citizen who'd arrested Unity had outlined the evidence against her, the man acting as judge turned to Unity. "Do you wish to speak?"

Fighting down a wave of fear, Unity stood and faced the twelve men. She briefly summarized her marriage to Whitley, the divorce, not mentioning that she'd given her child to her sister. She tried to explain why she didn't want the Whitleys to rear her child, but she was too embarrassed to speak of Samuel's base life-style.

"My family had taught me to respect God and to live as the Bible taught. The Whitleys were thieves and had made their fortune by preying on others." Her words seemed to influence the jurymen, whom Unity took to be God-fearing men.

"When I learned that my former husband was alive and here in the gold fields, I feared for the safety of my child. I sent the boy away with his nurse, when Samuel found out about him, but he continued to follow me, thinking I'd lead him to the boy. However much justification I may have had, I *did not* kill the man." Noticing the sympathetic faces before her, as she finished, Unity decided she had little to fear.

The jury didn't even leave the room to discuss the issue; they simply huddled together. In a matter of minutes, they turned to the judge. "Release the woman. We find her 'not guilty,' " one man said.

No sooner had the words been spoken than running steps sounded on the plank sidewalk. A man stuck his head into the door, shouting, "Fire! Fire! The whole town is ablaze. We need men for a bucket brigade."

The room emptied, with men jostling against one another in the small door. A few of the jurymen took time to shake hands with Matt and Unity, but soon they were alone, in each other's arms.

"Praise be to God," Matt cried, his voice breaking. "I've never been so fearful in my life."

Unity returned his kiss and then moved out of his arms. "Let's check on the fire. This could mean disaster to the city."

Smoke stung their eyes as soon as they stepped outside. Black waves billowed above the town, and burning embers shot through the dark clouds. Several bucket brigades had already formed from the bay to the center of the fire. As yet the blaze seemed a long way from the waterfront, but it could travel rapidly.

Alex stood in the door of Spencer Shipping, looking toward the burning city. He gave a joyous shout when he saw that Unity was free, but his concerned look returned immediately. "I've been trying to decide whether to go and help or stay here, in case the fire heads this way."

"You stay here with Unity and be on guard for looters," Matt said. "I'll go uptown and help as soon as I tell Sid to pull the *Allegheny* away from the wharf."

In spite of the smoke that stung their eyes, Alex and Unity spent most of the day in front of the warehouse, monitoring the progress of the fire. Anxiously they noticed that the blaze had reached the waterfront and that smoke poured from the windows of many businesses. Even from a distance they could feel the intense heat. Roofs collapsed, sending sparks high into the heavens. Explosions ripped through the area, so powerful that Unity fell to the ground.

"I'll wager blasting powder meant for the gold mines is causing the explosions," Alex said.

In mid-afternoon, Matt slipped away from the fire. "I'm needed up there, but I had to see how you were doing."

"Is the whole town going to burn?"

"I don't think so, but I've never experienced anything like this. Thousands of people try to stop the fire, but others run into burning stores, taking everything they can. It's commonly believed that the hoodlums started this, just to have a chance to loot and pillage." His face and hands were blackened, his clothes scorched where flying cinders had touched his back. "I think you're safe enough here, but stay alert."

By nightfall, though a few fires still burned, for the most part the city had been saved.

Matt coaxed Unity to take a carriage ride the next morning, but would not explain their destination. To her surprise, he drove to the hill where their newly completed house stood.

From the carriage they looked down on the city. It seemed to Unity that the whole center of the city and much of the waterfront was destroyed.

"Is this the end of San Francisco, Matt?"

He laughed. "No, listen." She could hear the restless stamping of the horses's feet, but nothing else significant at first, until the sound of hammers and saws drifted toward them.

"They're already building again.

"Somewhere I heard a myth about a beautiful bird called a phoenix that lived for hundreds of years, and after consuming itself in fire, it rose again from the ashes. I sorta figure Frisco is going to be a phoenix."

He laughed fondly. "I've wandered a good many years, but I've found home at last." Looking intently at Unity, he continued, humbly, "I feel as if *I've* been self-destructed. I had to go through the fire to claim you as my own, Unity, but I love you, and I think you're going to like the new Matt Miller. I can hardly believe how badly I treated you, but I'll never do it again. Will you marry me? This time nothing will come between us."

Her hands on his shoulders drew him near. "I'm a new person, too, Matt. I know what it means to turn away from mistakes and start again. God's given us a second chance; of course I'll marry you."

Together they toured the house. As they stood on the front porch, looking toward the city, Matt said, "The house only lacks one thing, Unity. A family. Let's go fetch Levi."

Unity kissed him. "I can hardly wait for our new life together. I know you never wanted to be engaged so long. Let's marry as soon as we can. Then we can bring Levi to our home."

"John won't like it if we aren't married at the ranch."

"But he said he'd need a month's notice, and I want to be married now. He can have a big celebration later, even if we aren't married there."

The expression on Matt's face was mystifying. "I can't believe that everything is turning out so well for me. It seems as if I've been fighting an uphill battle ever since my father died. It's hard to comprehend that I've finally reached the summit."

"You've been fighting against the tide, Matt, instead of flowing with it. God's tide of time has a way of washing away many problems."

When they returned to San Francisco, a boy was distributing copies of *The Nugget*, and Matt stopped the carriage to buy a copy of the newssheet. After they shared the evening meal, he settled down to read the paper's account of the fire. The damage had been extensive, but the editor expressed the opinion that San Francisco would rise above this defeat into an even greater city.

"Unity!"

Matt's call brought Unity running from the kitchen, where she'd been helping Jiang clear away the supper's dishes.

"Look at this!" he shouted excitedly. He pointed to a short news item at the bottom of the first page. She sat beside him to read the fine print:

Considering the extent of the conflagration, the loss of life was minimal; however, one death served to clear up a mystery surrounding one of the city's latest crimes. Micah Dilcher, late of Massachusetts, was mortally injured when the wall of a burning building crashed over him. On his deathbed, Dilcher admitted to the murder of Samuel Whitley, saying that he had arranged the body of his victim in a manner to throw suspicion upon one of San Francisco's leading merchants. Apparently the deceased left no survivors.

Unity threw her arms around Matt. "What if he had died without admitting that? The crime would have hung over my head the rest of my life. Will you go buy another copy of this newssheet, Matt? I feel that the least I can do would be to send Samuel's parents the notice of his death. Otherwise they'll be looking for him to come home. He told me that he'd written to them when he finally escaped from the Spanish captain who'd enslaved him."

"Will you tell them about Levi?"

"You know, I'll have to pray about that. Surely they should know their own grandson, but would they try to take him from me? He's *my* son—our son—and surely the Lord would want me to see he's brought up in a godly family. Someday, in God's own time, we may see reconciliation. But is *now* that time?"

Matt simply held her close.

A cold, misty rain fell on the newlyweds, all the way to the rancho, but despite the weather, when they arrived on the summit overlooking the Pacific, Unity said, "Let's go down to the beach."

They tethered their horses and pack animals and dismounted to walk hand in hand along the shore. The receding tide was boisterous, and the waves wafted spray toward them. Unity held her face toward the water, savoring the full force of the ocean. She stooped to pick up a colorful shell, but the foamy wave swirling around her feet snatched it from her hand and carried it seaward.

Laughing, she said, "The tides of time wash over my soul. It seems as if I've been lashed by strong waves ever since I married Samuel. My life has been turbulent, tempestuous. High tides came when Levi was born and when I fell in love with you. I've suffered low tides, but now they've risen again. Just the way these waves have carried the shells and other debris away, God has purged my life, Matt."

"All the dross is gone, you mean?"

"Yes. Life has a way of treating us that way. No matter how much we fret, God's cleansing waves finally come. I love you, my husband, and I thank our Lord that He brought us together."

A towering wave approached, and Matt pulled her backward just in time to keep them from being submerged. With his slow laugh, he said, "In the past few months, I've had many of life's big waves, and I suppose we'll have more. But as long as we're together, I can face them."

"We'll be together, Matt, I promise you that."